NO MORE HEARTACHE

Books by Evelyn Claire

NO MORE HEARTACHE
STORM REMEMBERED

NO MORE HEARTACHE

EVELYN CLAIRE

DOUBLEDAY & COMPANY, INC.
GARDEN CITY, NEW YORK
1986

All of the characters in this book
are fictitious, and any resemblance
to actual persons, living or dead,
is purely coincidental.

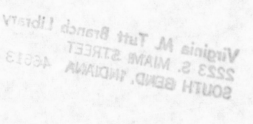
Library of Congress Cataloging-in-Publication Data

Claire, Evelyn.
No more heartache.

I. Title.
PS3553.L223N6   1986   813'.54
ISBN 0-385-23189-X

Library of Congress Catalog Card Number 85-16303
Copyright © 1986 by Evelyn Claire
All Rights Reserved
Printed in the United States of America
First Edition

NO MORE HEARTACHE

CHAPTER ONE

"Lee, look what's just come! Another delivery from Neiman's. Lee?"

Lee Colder was at her desk, one hand on the telephone she had just put down, the other making notations on a paper before her. The desk was piled with more sheets, scattered and random. Lee's red-gold hair fell forward, hiding her face as she wrote furiously.

"Ed Ackerman in Pittsburgh," she said. "Do you know I couldn't even get him to come to the phone last month? Now he's calling us."

"Yes, I know, but look at this, Lee." Buffie Simmons stood in the doorway of Lee's office, her hands on her substantial hips, pencil stuck through her untidy gray hair. A stack of cartons was behind her. She was glaring at Lee over her reading glasses. "I think these are lamps. *I* don't know where they go. You'll have to decide."

"Oh, Buffie"—Lee sank back in her chair and flung her hair over her shoulders—"I'm so tired!"

"I know, honey. Why don't you take a little break? And look over these things while you're at it," Buffie added.

"No, I'm not tired—that's not it." Lee tapped her even white teeth with her pencil. "I'm just fed up."

"Sure you are, I don't wonder," Buffie agreed sympathetically, ready to fall in with Lee's mood no matter how capricious. Buffie had been accountant, bookkeeper, and supervisor of copyrights at the WW Music Company since its founding fifteen years before and was the closest friend motherless Lee had known since babyhood.

"It's just so—so unfair!" Lee exploded. Her wide green eyes

shot sparks of resentment, and a flush of color tinged her creamy skin. "They all know WW Music's been sold—everybody read it in *Billboard* last week. And now the distributors and even the radio stations are falling all over themselves to be nice to us."

Buffie shrugged. "Might as well enjoy it, honey."

Lee sighed and was silent for a moment. Then she said softly, "It's not mine any more, Buffie. WW Music belongs to the Camerons now."

"All right, no more of that talk. You did what you had to do. You didn't let the company go under. There's still going to be a WW Music, and that's what your daddy would have wanted."

"Maybe. But who knows what they're going to do to it?"

"Oh fiddle. What can they do? Nothing but improve it, I'll bet."

"You're no more sure of that than I am," Lee said accusingly. "Who knows what the Camerons will think of—with all their millions?"

Buffie gave a little shrug. "I guess we'll start finding out tomorrow when Mr. Cameron gets here. Now what about these lamps? I suppose they're for his private office."

"No doubt," Lee said bitterly.

"Well, what shall I—"

"Oh, who cares? Sort them out any way you like, Buffie. Let the great man rearrange them himself if he's not satisfied."

"The painters have cleared out finally," Buffie said, and added cautiously, "Wouldn't you like to take a look?"

"No, I wouldn't," Lee glowered. "Besides, I'm swamped here. Is Steve back?"

"Somebody looking for me?" Steve Harper loomed up behind Buffie, grinning and in obvious good spirits, his red hair curling tightly all over his head, his big wraparound glasses catching glints of light. Steve was seldom out of sorts, rarely anything but enthusiastic, and now, despite the gloom of her own thoughts, Lee was glad to see him.

"Did you go to KCM?"

"Yep, here in Dallas, and I went to radio stations in Fort

Worth too while I was at it. Red-carpet treatment all the way. They're anxious to play anything we send them."

Because of his red hair, which was more violent in tone than Lee's, Steve was often taken for her brother, and in fact he was as close to her as a brother. They were the same age, twenty-six, and he had been, along with Buffie, her loyal mainstay since Dub Colder's death five years before. The faltering company had been dumped into Lee's unprepared lap.

"That's what I've been getting," Lee said sourly, glancing at the telephone. "A whole morning of it. I was just talking to Delta Distributors in New York. And they called *me*, if you can believe it. Full of smiles and blandishments and wanted to hear all about any new releases we might have."

"Smiles and *blandishments?*" Steve echoed. "I'm not even sure what those are. And you couldn't be sure about the smiles, could you? I mean, on the phone."

"Oh, you know what I mean." Lee gave her hair a toss. "I could hear it in their voices. What about you? You must be running into the same thing if you got good treatment at KCM. They were certainly cold-shouldering us up until last week."

"Oh sure. But I'm not knocking it. What's so bad about getting some good treatment for a change? After five years of me pleading to get our new releases on the air, and then you trying to collect our money from the distributors—what's so bad about it?"

"And that's another thing," Lee exploded. "They're all paying their bills!"

Buffie, who saw the world through a haze of red ink and black, intervened. "I'm with Steve. What's so terrible about having some of those accounts paid up?"

Lee sighed. "Nothing, I guess. Only when the company belonged to us"—she always thought of it as the three of them —"they didn't care how long they made us wait. And we had to plead with them to take our new releases. Now they want everything we can send them and they're promising prompt

payment. Everyone wanting to stand in well with the Camerons and their money."

She glanced from one face to the other, reading perplexity
in both of them, and admitted to herself that she was being
irrational. And was she, when you came right down to it, being
completely honest? Wasn't it a relief not to have to worry
anymore about a stack of bills each month? Wasn't it good not
to have to spend her every waking moment worrying about
the future of the company? To turn it all over to other hands
and to sleep soundly at night once more? Yes to all that. But
another anxiety gnawed at her and gave her moments of cold
apprehension. She had been asked to stay on with the company, and she had quickly insisted that she would need Buffie
and Steve because of their experience. But would the new
owner—the giant conglomerate Cambro—care about small
provisions lightly agreed to? Steve was young and eager—he
could no doubt find a place with another record company, but
Buffie—what would she do if she were let go?

"Hey, relax," Steve said, studying her face. "Why don't we
wait until tomorrow and see what happens?"

"Oh, I suppose you're right."

"And look, honey," said Buffie in a low voice, "it's done now.
Whatever happens happens. We've got to live with it. We
couldn't have gone on as we were, now could we?"

"I know." Lee nodded agreement, but she was finding it
suddenly difficult to speak. She looked up at the picture that
faced her from the wall opposite her desk: a huge poster-sized
photograph of her father, Dub Colder, as he had looked at the
height of his popularity fifteen years before, the same year he
had started the WW Music Company. Wallace Wesley Colder
—never called anything but Dub—whose original singing and
songwriting had catapulted him into nationwide popularity
and who had, along with a handful of other singers, raised
country music to a status competitive in prestige with other
popular music, paving the way for the rise of dozens of country
artists who came after him. In the photograph the big Western
hat was tilted back rakishly, the eyes sparkled, the familiar

guitar rested easily against his body. It was a pose Lee loved; it was the way she remembered her father best.

"But oh, Dub," she addressed the well-loved features under her breath. "If only you'd been one quarter the businessman that you were a singer!" And yet she knew in her secret heart that it was his goodness, his generosity that had been Dub's undoing. No down-and-out singer from his past life was ever turned away from WW Music. Dub would always manage to dig up the money to finance a recording session for him. And invariably the record would prove to be a flop. No country musician he had ever toured with was refused a handout when his luck went sour. Warmhearted and sympathetic, Dub had let the company trickle away in small generosities until only his own catalog of popular hits was sustaining it, and it was not enough. Then, seeing what was happening yet feeling himself powerless to change it, he had begun to drink—a little at first, later a lot. Here Lee's memories veered off and stopped. She did not want to remember all that—only the good part.

She took a deep breath and looked again at Steve and Buffie, both of them watching her, waiting to take their cue from her. Resolutely Lee pushed herself up from her desk and forced cheerfulness into her tone.

"Okay, let's take a look at these darned lamps, Buffie," she grinned.

The suite of offices engaged by the Cameron company in its first gesture toward expansion adjoined the old offices of WW Music, and the two were a study in contrasts. The new offices, just vacated by the decorators, had carpeting of soft creamy beige covering all the floors. A complementary color had been chosen for the walls, where the work of several famous Southwestern artists hung, along with an Indian rug of subdued desert hues. The furniture, of leather and tweed, was in earth tones of ochre and russet, suggestive of the Texas landscape itself. The whole office was sophisticated in style yet completely comfortable. It made all the more stark the run-down state of the old offices next door, where paint peeled and wires were mended with electrician's tape, where posters of country singers curled at the corners, and where an ancient coffee maker chugged and sputtered amid a scattering of Styrofoam cups. But *that's* WW Music, not this, Lee thought as she went through the door to examine with a resentful eye the glossy new suite and its freight of expensive office equipment, eight-foot desk of gleaming mahogany, chairs that swiveled and reclined.

For a moment she stood there in her denim skirt, boots, and Western-style silk blouse, glaring with disapproval at the job the decorators had done.

"It looks like the lobby of the new Dallas Hilton," she said sourly. "All that's missing is the swimming pool."

"Oh come on, honey, what's wrong with it?" Buffie panted, following her in and dragging a carton behind her. "There's nothing wrong with sprucing up a little. We really have let things run down. I suppose that's how Mr. Cameron felt."

"Or maybe he was just worried about his own comfort, moving from his plush Chicago office. And I'm sure he didn't want to mingle with the natives. You notice he reserved this nice new suite for himself, away from the rest of us."

"Well, of course he'll be meeting lots of people—first impressions count in business, you know," Buffie answered vaguely. She had leaned over and was busy opening the carton. Lee, with a sudden pang of tenderness and concern, noticed the older woman's flyaway hair, sagging hemline, and sturdy shoes. If first impressions counted in Ben Cameron's world of glitter and hype, then Buffie herself would certainly not fit in. Lee made a sudden promise to herself. If she goes, I go. And Mr. Ben Megabuck Cameron can just figure his own way around WW Music.

"Oh, Lee, isn't that the handsomest thing! Look at that!" Buffie had removed from the carton a Stiffel lamp with a brass base and a tweed-textured ivory shade. "And look, here's another one like it—well no, not exactly the same. And there are three more cartons. Let's see what's in them." Buffie scrambled and pulled. "Lee, look, these have ceramic bases. Oh, I love this one with the brown and beige swirls. They all look too nice for an office!"

"Not for Mr. Cameron's office, I'm sure."

"Well, he should have nice things—it's his company now," Buffie said, and then at once rushed on, "Oh dear, I shouldn't have said that, Lee. I didn't mean—you know, it's just that—if you have all that money, I suppose you might as well spend it."

"I know, Buffie," Lee sighed. "No apologies necessary. Come on, let's start figuring where to put these things." She picked up the Stiffel with the tweed shade and plunked it down on the gleaming desk next to the electronic speaker phone that had just been installed. "How about right there?"

Buffie stood back and put her head to one side. "Yes. Very nice. And perhaps the swirly one on that table against the wall. But to the left of the painting, of course, so as not to hide it."

"I don't really see why he needs any of them—he's put in all those recessed ceiling spots and dimmers."

"Well, lamps make it cosier, I suppose. . . ."

"Is there an electrical outlet under this desk?"

"I'm sure there is, yes."

"I don't see it. You don't suppose the carpet people covered it, do you?"

"Goodness, they wouldn't have done that, would they?"

"Wait a minute, I'll get under there and see."

In Lee's own office, far off, the telephone was ringing. She heard Steve answer it.

"Oh dear, maybe I'd better give him a hand," Buffie worried.

"He can manage for a few minutes. Let's get this job done." Lee was on her hands and knees now, crawling under the huge desk. "It's as big as the Astrodome under here," she complained irritably. "At least we'll know where to hide next time there's a tornado watch. The whole company can fit under here very nicely."

"Honestly, Lee. . . ."

"What I can't figure out is why this Cameron feels he has to come down here and take charge personally. Of course the

lawyer who took care of the sale for them did hint that what
they were planning was a lot bigger than just turning one little
music company around. Did you know they're building their
own recording studio too? I mean, the latest in everything!
Twenty-four-track recording and a computer board that I
hear is an engineer's dream. What I think is that they're really
planning on starting themselves a little entertainment empire
down here. And of course this Ben Cameron is the youngest of
the three brothers, so maybe he doesn't count for much. I
mean, maybe they're just sending him down here to keep him
out of their hair. There's one like that in every family, you
know. Hey, here it is! I've found it. Just hand me that wire now,
Buffie."

Silence answered her.

"Buffie?"

From under the small space at the base of the desk the lamp
cord was pushed toward Lee. "This what you're looking for?"
asked an unfamiliar male voice.

Lee scrambled backward so suddenly she narrowly missed
banging her head on the desk. She stood up, flushed and rumpled, to confront a tall stranger who stood smiling at her across
the polished wood surface.

"Who . . ." she began uncertainly, searching his brilliant
blue eyes for some clue to his identity.

"Ben Cameron," the man said smoothly. "The one who
doesn't count for much?"

Lee could feel an embarrassed flush spreading over her face.
Her throat had suddenly closed so tightly that she could not
get a word out. The blue eyes were looking at her with amusement.

"I'm sorry," she managed to stammer at last. "But we expected you tomorrow!" It came out sounding like a wail.
"Things aren't done around here, and we would have been
prepared—I mean, we would have arranged to greet you
properly—that is—" She broke off and stood there helplessly,
taking in the dark hair, the broad shoulders in the exquisitely
tailored suit. He wore no jewelry except for a slim gold watch

of European style which she glimpsed under the edge of a smooth cuff.

He seemed to take no notice of her confusion beyond being mildly entertained by it. "I just decided there was no point in waiting, and I was anxious to be here and settled in so that we could get things moving." His mouth had quirked up on one side and she thought he was enjoying her discomfort.

"I'd have appreciated it if you'd let us know," she said with all the dignity she could muster considering the fact that her blouse had pulled out at the waist and her hair was rumpled and out of place, one strand hanging down in front of her eyes.

"I am sorry. But I'm sure Miss Colder will forgive me when she knows that it was all in the interest of the company. Will she be in soon?"

Now it was Lee's turn to feel a faint brush of amusement. "I'm Lee Colder," she said.

If she had hoped to disconcert him, she did not succeed. His pleasant expression never faltered. He extended his hand across the desk.

"Miss Colder. So happy we've met at last. They told me you did everything around here," he added with a twinkle. "Now I can believe it."

His handshake was warm and firm, but it served only to increase Lee's discomfort. It seemed to communicate to her so much poise, so much assurance, and perhaps something more. It carried with it the magnetism of the successful male—the man accustomed to getting his own way. Probably with women as well as in everything else, Lee told herself.

"Anyway, I do apologize," she said with difficulty, and withdrew her hand. "I mean, I shouldn't have said that about you." She could still feel the pressure of his touch.

"Certainly not before meeting me," he murmured. "Afterward, perhaps." He glanced around the office. "And things do seem to be in reasonably good shape here. Nothing much left to do, I'd say." His eyes swung back to her. "Perhaps I should apologize too, for barging in on you like that. But in the office out there phones were ringing and everyone seemed busy, and so I just wandered in on my own."

"It's your office," Lee said, and in spite of herself could not quite keep the hard edge out of her voice.

"Yes, of course. So it is. I'm not quite used to the idea yet."

It was impossible, Lee thought, to fault him anywhere. Everything he said was so perfectly courteous and correct. And oddly she found herself resenting this as much as anything else about him. His polite, deferential attitude was as much an irritant to her as arrogance would have been, since it seemed to offer no toehold for her own animosity. Prepared to resent him, she found no grievance to get hold of. Briefly it occurred to her that he might be doing it for that very reason.

"Well then," she said, trying to recover something from the situation, "perhaps I could show you around?"

"Wonderful, I'd like that. Only as long as I'm here, why don't we start by getting the staff together? I'd like very much to meet the people I'll be working with."

"Certainly," Lee said. She stepped to the office door and spoke to the others, then turned back, tucking in her blouse and brushing the strand of hair from her face. She folded her arms in front of her and let her trim hundred and ten pounds rest on one leg in an attitude of casual waiting. Buffie and Steve edged in, looking puzzled and eyeing the newcomer warily. Buffie's glasses had slipped down again and Steve's red curls were sticking out militantly.

"Well, here we are, Mr. Cameron," Lee said with a wry smile. "This *is* WW Music."

He was studying her curiously, and there was no way now, Lee thought, that he could avoid reading her resentment.

CHAPTER TWO

"Please sit down, won't you?" Ben Cameron said politely after Lee had performed the introductions. "Here, Buffie—you don't mind if I call you Buffie? Try this chair." He escorted her by a gentle pressure on her elbow to one of the russet leather chairs, where she sank down, utterly charmed and bewildered. "Steve, make yourself comfortable."

Lee hurried to take a seat before he could get to her. She had no desire to be the object of what she regarded as the manufactured Cameron charm. She sat quite straight, and her arms stayed folded defiantly. Ben Cameron sat on the edge of the big desk and let one foot swing lightly in its polished cordovan leather. She saw his glance rest on her and she returned the look levelly, even though it was difficult when she could feel the scrutiny of those blue eyes, as tangible almost as the touch of his hand would have been. But she was determined not to be overawed by him, as she was sure most women were.

"Well, you know now that I'm Ben Cameron," he said pleasantly. "And the very first thing I want to say to you is that I'm happy to be here in Dallas, but I'm going to need plenty of help from all three of you. I'm no stranger to business, but this isn't ball bearings or iron foundries or oil wells, or even the airline or hotel business. I know something about those, but the music business is new to me. I'll be feeling my way, learning every day. And I know I can count on all of you to point out my mistakes to me." He paused and smiled suddenly at Lee. It was a smile that caused crinkles to appear at the corners of his eyes and that gave his face a look of mischief and fun. She ignored it deliberately, feeling sure it was a ploy he had used before with great effectiveness.

"If you're wondering," he went on, "why an organization like Cambro has taken an interest in acquiring a relatively small company such as WW Music, I'll tell you. It's because this is a firm of such traditional reputation and prestigious name that we feel it's an ideal point from which to launch our plans for this area. I'm sure you already know," he added with another pointed look at Lee, "that we are building our own studio here in Dallas. We feel that will give us a good nucleus for the new ventures in recording that we plan to embark on. We see the possibilities as limitless. And we're not ruling out films in the future either. The music-video market is something we're now exploring."

He looked around at the three of them, all looking so out of place in the plush office, and said with a glint of amusement, "I was going to assure you right at the start that no one would be let go in our reorganization process. Now I see that I not only couldn't do without any of you, but that it will be necessary to hire an even larger staff. However, I will be counting on you three to guide me every step of the way. First of all, I think salary adjustments commensurate with the load of work you'll be carrying should be made. We'll meet separately to discuss all that beginning tomorrow morning. And defining your jobs should go along with it. Miss Colder—Lee"—he said her name with an intimacy that implied they were already friends—"I know how much responsibility you've been carrying. From now on you will be senior vice president in charge of marketing and national merchandising. Steve, what kind of duties have you had?"

"Mostly arm-twisting," Steve grinned. "Trying to get the DJ's to play our releases. And you know, publicity, promotion, that kind of thing."

"Fine. You'll be manager of press and public information. And Buffie?"

Buffie pushed her glasses up nervously by the nosepiece.

"Why, I'm the bookkeeper, Mr. Cameron, and I keep track of the copyrights."

Ben Cameron gave a small wave of one well-manicured hand. "We'll hire someone to take care of that. And the new computer we're getting will do most of it anyway. I'd like you to supervise all of it, however. You'll be our director of operations and business administration. And as one of your first jobs, will you see about hiring me a private secretary tomorrow? I don't want to add to anyone's workload, certainly. And we'll need a receptionist too."

Very neat, Lee thought. Raises for all hands and fancy, meaningless titles designed to flatter. Yet she had to admit he had handled it skillfully. Steve was glowing with importance and Buffie looked ready to melt into a puddle of gratitude. There was no denying that he had done a tactful thing—making Buffie feel necessary and at the same time giving her the job of hiring new people, so that instead of feeling pushed aside she became a part of the whole scheme of expansion. And Steve was obviously ready to stand on his head to win approval from his new boss. All well and good for those two, Lee thought. Certainly there was no need for it with me. I'm not waiting for anyone to throw me a bone. No doubt that was the kind of thing Ben Cameron was used to doing—handling people, manipulating them for his own ends. She glanced at him and saw that he was giving her such a piercing, direct look that she reddened slightly, fearing he might be reading her thoughts.

"Let me also reassure you that we have no plans to do away with anything at present," he went on. "Only to bring in new ideas and new, exciting artists. And Steve, as your first release to the press, you'll be announcing the signing of Nikki North and Joe Bud Garrett."

He paused to let this announcement sink in, and if he had hoped to surprise and impress, Lee had to admit he had succeeded. Looks of astonishment darted among the three of them as they realized the import of what he was saying. Joe Bud Garrett was a veteran country singer, his career studded with gold records. Nikki North was a rising star who had recently teamed up with him for a new album and a number of concert appearances. Her career was definitely headed upward. If Ben Cameron had succeeded in coaxing them away from the Nashville company for which they had been recording, it was a fairly noteworthy feat. It was also, to Lee, faintly disturbing, for North and Garrett were now middle-of-the-road singers, crossover stars, both terms used in the business to describe singers who had turned from a traditional country style to adopt a more popular, mass-market approach to singing. Nothing wrong with that, of course, Lee told herself, trying to be reasonable, except that it was so completely different from the simple, genuine sort of singing that her father had done and which had always formed the backbone of WW Music's catalog. There was a glossiness about it that spoke of elaborate studios, special effects, voices improved electronically, manipulated by a control board and by engineering which took much of the originality and feeling out of it so that in the end what resulted was more product than artistry in her opinion.

Ben Cameron's voice cut through the stunned silence in the office. "Sound good to you?" He was addressing all of them, but his eyes were fixed on Lee's face.

"Hey, that's great, Mr. Cameron!" Steve exploded. "I'll get going on the press releases right away."

Buffie had closed her eyes, thinking hard. "Nikki North," she said. "Nikki North. Why, I remember her. She's from around here somewhere. Grand Prairie, I believe. She won a contest once—Miss Metroplex. I think her name was Nola Mae Nettles."

Ben Cameron's eyes widened. *"Brava,* Buffie," he said heartily. "I can see that encyclopedic memory is going to come in handy. Miss Colder—Lee—how do you feel about it?" A slightly sardonic note had crept into his voice.

Lee sat up straighter and let her hands sink to her lap. "It sounds like quite a triumph of persuasion on your part, Mr. Cameron."

"Please make it Ben."

"Only it occurs to me—that is, it seems apparent that you plan to change the direction of the company."

"How so?"

"Well, Garrett and North are big crossover pop stars. What they do couldn't really be described as country music, could it?"

"You're the expert on that, of course," he replied easily. "What *my* expertise tells me is that they are singers who have been showing a profit on every release and they are a highly effective act visually, a good thing to keep in mind for our future music-video plans. As to changing the direction of WW Music—yes, I suppose I do plan to change it—in the direction of showing a profit. Any objections to that?"

"No, of course not." Even as Lee struggled to keep the bitterness out of her voice, she could not help being impressed with the way he had done it. Garrett and North were major recording stars, no denying it. But then, she thought, the three Cameron brothers were often linked in the press with glamorous show people, entertaining them in their many homes, appearing in celebrity golf tournaments and other charity affairs with them. Probably there was no trick at all to it when you had all that charm and money at your command. She thought of the last five years and the struggle she had had trying to keep the company solvent. Two stars like that would have saved us, she thought. But now handsome Ben Cameron, stepping into the country music field almost as into a new hobby, had overnight bought himself a record company, built a glittering new studio, and signed two highly profitable stars. Waving his checkbook like a magic wand, he had accomplished it overnight, and now WW Music was well on the way to becoming a different kind of company, with no resemblance to the one her father had founded.

"Lee?" His voice cut into her thoughts.

"I'm sorry."

"I was about to say," he went on quietly, "that you must surely realize that Dub Colder's sound was new too when he started his career. No one had ever sung country music in quite that way before. There's nothing wrong with changing with the times, is there?"

"Surely you're not comparing this kind of—of glossy commercialism to Dub's music."

Still quietly disarming, Ben said, "I can only answer that by saying that if we still had artists of Dub Colder's caliber, there'd probably be no need for change. But as it is—"

"Isn't quality always in style?" Lee asked hotly.

He gave her a penetrating look. "I'm afraid I have to answer that by saying—" He hesitated and she thought he was choosing his words carefully. Then he went on, "By saying that I consider it important to go with today's sound. The company must be brought up to a paying basis."

She had no answer, and his determined patience had left her weaponless. What rejoinder could there be to such an eminently sensible argument? Wasn't that after all why she had sold WW Music in the first place? Wasn't it the hope of salvaging something out of the wreck of the company that had prompted her? How could she possibly argue with what he was trying to do?

"Nikki and Joe Bud will be arriving here next week," he went on smoothly. "I have reserved the San Carlos Hotel for a big reception for them on the twentieth. There's a lot to do to prepare for that. I have the plans roughed in, but I'll need help from all of you. Especially with the guest list. Lee, you'll give me a hand with that, I hope. We'll be inviting disk jockeys, newspaper people—we'll want television coverage, of course. But then also we'll ask important local people. The mayor, city officials, people who are active socially. And Nikki and Joe Bud will be doing their part too. They'll make an appearance, do a show for charity at the hotel that weekend. All by way of publicizing our new studio, the Cambro Park area where it's located, indeed the whole operation. We want the whole country to be aware of it—and them."

"Of course. We'll all be glad to help," Lee said crisply. "Any guidelines on what we should spend? Around here we're rather aware of that."

Ben Cameron hesitated only momentarily, then said coolly, "No, none. Spend whatever you need to make it a success. And good publicity—that's important to us at this stage."

In the outer office a telephone shrilled again and Lee, glad for an excuse to escape, jumped to her feet.

"I'd better start tending to business," she said. "If you'll excuse me?" She hurried out and took care of the call. Buffie, following after her moments later with a look of lingering excitement, leaned over the desk as Lee hung up and said, "He's very nice, isn't he, Lee? I mean, there really wasn't anything to worry about, was there?"

"I'm sure we'll get along," Lee said, unwilling to spoil Buffie's mood by saying what she really thought—that Ben Cameron had descended on WW Music like the strong wind of a blue norther, the wild north wind that could change the balmy Texas air in a matter of hours to stinging cold. Except—Lee's essential, bone-deep honesty forced her to admit it—things hadn't been what you could call really balmy around here for the last five years, or even before that.

"Miss Colder?" She looked up with a start, and Buffie moved away toward her own desk as Ben Cameron approached. He leaned forward, putting both hands flat on the desktop and looking very directly at her, his face only inches from hers. She could catch the subtle scent that clung around him—the indefinable aura of wealth, she thought—good fabric, expensive shaving lotion, good leather, good grooming—darn Ben Cameron and his money anyway!

"Yes, Mr. Cameron?" His nearness was making her uneasy, out of control. She longed to put more distance between them.

"Ah, I see it's still Mr. Cameron," he said regretfully. "I was hoping you'd call me Ben. I can't really keep calling you Lee unless you do, you see."

"I'm sorry if I—"

"I've always heard Texans are such warm, friendly people."

"They are, of course. That is, we are."

"I'll have to take your word for that."

The piercing blue eyes were boring so deep into hers that Lee could not evade them. And now she could see a soft flickering in them that was like light upon moving water, making them look suddenly less sharp and businesslike. Maybe, she thought hesitantly, maybe it was just possible that he did want to be friendly. And if so, wasn't she being unforgivably distant and rigid?

"I'm sorry," she said at last. "I didn't mean to give the impression—that is, perhaps I've been too—"

"Let's start over," he said smoothly. "How about it?"

She gave a small nod and managed a smile, aware that her heart was pounding unaccountably.

"And how about lunch?" he asked.

"Oh really, I have a ton of work to take care of here, and I usually just have a sandwich at my desk."

"Then today let's do what's not usual," he said easily. "In honor of my arrival. How about it? We can even go on talking business if it'll make you feel better."

She hesitated a moment longer, trying to slow the thumping of her heart. Then her shoulders came up in a small shrug. She dreaded being alone with him. She longed to be able to turn the clock back. She wished she could just say no, or even repeat a secret charm or spell that would bring it all back the way it had been only a short time ago when the company had been hers and there had been no one to answer to. Even with all the smothering problems, the choking mountain of bills each month— She stopped herself from thinking further, knowing she was being foolish. It was just that this was such a new experience, she told herself; it had come too fast. But it was done now and there could be no turning back. She squared her shoulders and took a deep breath.

"You're the boss," she said.

He drove to a small French restaurant in the exclusive Turtle Creek area near Highland Park.

"It's the only place I've been able to find my way to in the short time I've been here," he admitted with a laugh.

"Are you staying nearby?" she asked, trying to make polite conversation.

"Yes, the company owns a condominium here—Turtle Creek, that is. I'm using it at least for the time being. But I think you'll like this place."

Reluctantly Lee had to admit to herself that it was just the sort of place that did appeal to her. There was a country-French look about it—hardwood floors, wooden tables with blue print cloths and napkins, hutches displaying Quimper ware. A far cry, she thought wryly, from the old Tolbert's Chili House, which she was more familiar with and which had been famous for its legendary chili. Well-dressed men and women occupied most of the tables here. Successful business people and executives, Lee guessed.

A quietly efficient waiter brought them canapés of smoked salmon and caviar, followed by a pheasant and truffle salad, beef tenderloin with foie gras, raspberry tarts, and white wine.

"Do you eat like this all the time?" she could not help asking at last. "I mean, how does anybody do business in the afternoon after all this? Not to mention the problems of staying a normal size." She glanced at his trim, muscular physique.

He smiled at her a little sheepishly. "I'm afraid I was trying to make a good impression," he admitted. "I thought I didn't exactly get off on the right foot with you." He waited for the waiter to pour their coffee and then he looked at her across the gleaming white china and silver, the blue print cloth. He said in a quiet voice, "Why do you resent me so much, Lee? Don't we have the same goals—to make WW Music prosperous again?"

Lee sipped her coffee, which was dark and delicious. She eyed him over the rim of her cup. "Yes, of course the same goals," she said hesitantly. "Only perhaps the means we would choose to achieve them are different."

He said slowly and tactfully, "I have a fairly good track record, you know, when it comes to turning failing companies around, making them pay their way again. Contrary to what you may have thought about my being sent down here to get out of my brothers' hair."

"Oh please," Lee said, reddening. "Don't remind me of those awful things I said."

"I don't think you consider them awful at all," he grinned. "Only awful that you got caught at it." She opened her mouth to protest, but he went on before she could answer. "But what I'm trying to tell you is that I want only the best for the company. And I don't want anyone—you most of all—to feel slighted or pushed aside. I'm sure we'll be able to work together well."

Reluctantly Lee said, "I do want to thank you for treating Buffie and Steve so fairly."

"I never planned to do otherwise," he said briskly. Then he moved on abruptly. "All right now. Tell me a little bit more about everyone. What about Buffie and Steve? Have they been with the company long?"

He was able to put subjects in pigeonholes, she thought, like someone tidying up a desk. This goes here, that goes there.

"Buffie's been with the company longer than anyone. When my father formed it, she was the first employee. She knows everything there is to know about WW Music and she knows pretty much everything about the music business in general."

"So do you, from what I hear."

She could not help wondering just what he had heard about her, but she could not bring herself to ask, nor did she want Ben Cameron to think it mattered to her in any way what he might be thinking about her, so she went on. "Steve came in as promotion man just before my father died. He always had a kind of hero-worship thing for Dub, I suspect. And he's good at what he does too. Also, he's a pretty fair singer himself. He gigs on weekends at local clubs, so he's always on the inside of the local music scene."

He was nodding slowly, concentrating on what she was saying. "What about you? When did you come into the company?"

"I'd helped out, on and off, whenever I could, but I really took over when Dub died." Telling it to him, trying to be matter-of-fact about it, Lee nevertheless felt a sudden pang of remembering, something she usually managed to keep at bay. But all of a sudden, there it was—the stark cleanliness and efficiency of the hospital room where Dub had died of pneumonia following those three days when no one had been able to find him. It was Steve and two of his musician friends who had finally located him in a seedy motel in Waco. By the time they got him to the hospital, they all knew he was past help.

"You had no one to advise you or help you?" Ben Cameron asked in a quiet voice.

"I had Buffie."

"But no one else."

"I had to make my own mistakes, if that's what you mean," Lee answered dryly, drawing back defensively from his sympathy. She could not bring herself to tell him what she now knew to be true, that no one could have saved WW Music at that point without investing a great deal of money. That Dub Colder had run it so far into the ground that there had been no chance of bringing it back with the limited resources she had had to work with. She sensed that Ben Cameron was getting ready to ask her about this aspect of the company's troubles, but she was determined not to discuss it with him. Dub's shortcomings were not a subject she cared to talk about with anyone, least of all a stranger, which this man still was, to her. Her father's place in the history of country music was secure, his talent legendary. No one was going to change that, Lee thought with fierce protectiveness.

"I'm going to get those painters back," he said casually, and Lee, bewildered at the change in subject, looked up from the table. His expression was bland, unrevealing.

"Painters?"

"Yes. I'll call the decorating firm myself. I didn't realize the rest of the office needed a face-lift as well. A little new furniture wouldn't hurt either."

"Oh really, that's not necessary, Mr.—Ben. We're quite used

to things as they are. It's perfectly all right." Lee found herself
in a state of uncomfortable confusion as she tried to keep up
with his changes and turns of mind. He seemed to jump from
one issue to another with complete ease.

"Oh, I think not," he said, still in that offhand way. "We need
to start looking prosperous right away. It'll help the way we
think, our attitude toward ourselves. That's important in business. Peeling paint looks like failure, and it makes us think
failure."

Lee, smarting under the implied criticism, said grimly,
"Well, no one could accuse you of thinking that way. Signing
North and Garrett certainly starts the new management of the
company off on a real up note."

He picked up a bread crumb from the tablecloth, rolled it
between long fingers, and dropped it. "You don't much like
the idea of their coming with WW Music, do you?"

"It's not up to me to like or not like anything anymore."

"Profit's the name of the game, Lee," he said in a firm voice.
"How about giving me a chance before judging me too severely?"

"Yes, of course," she said in a small voice. Why do I resent
him so much, she wondered, when he's making such an obvious effort to be pleasant and not make waves? Is it just personal
pique, because he's taken over something I've thought of as
my own for the last five years? Probably, she admitted helplessly. But underneath those thoughts, far back in a corner of
her mind, she seemed to feel the presence of a personality
different from the smooth facade that handsome Ben Cameron showed to the world. Was she only imagining it, or was
there really another Ben Cameron—a ruthless, iron-willed
one who had no intention of being crossed, in business or in
any other part of his life? Something struck Lee—a chill, a
shiver that had nothing to do with the quiet, unobtrusive air-
conditioning in the elegant restaurant. Something that felt
suspiciously like dread. And fear.

If that other Ben Cameron did exist, hidden away, secret,
well-concealed, how long, Lee wondered, would it be before
he showed himself?

CHAPTER THREE

Certainly, Lee had to admit, there was no sign of any such personality during the days that followed. Ben Cameron, his tie and jacket discarded, the sleeves of his custom-fitted shirt rolled up, worked alongside the rest of them as the office was pulled into shape—files reorganized, catalog notations brought up to date. He was agreeable to a fault, smiling and considerate. His efficiency was awesome; she could not help recognizing that. And he was endlessly patient, unfailingly courteous to her and the others. With one part of his attention he oversaw the installation of an impressive new computer in a special room set aside for it. With another part he offhandedly contracted for the decorators to return and do over the older part of the office where she and Buffie and Steve had their cubicles.

"What color do you like?" he asked, sticking his head inside her door the day after his arrival.

"What color?" she echoed blankly.

"Yes, for your office. I want to tell the decorators."

"Oh—I see—well, really, I don't—why don't you choose?" She felt totally helpless, out of her depth in the face of his self-assurance, his air of command.

"Okay," he said pleasantly, tilting his head to one side as though to study her. "I think perhaps peach—"

She felt herself blushing. "Fine. All right."

Later she heard him issuing orders to the decorating firm, and by the way he spoke she could tell that no detail was too small to escape his attention. Yet he seemed at the same time to be expert in delegating responsibility so that his own day was not cluttered with matters which others could be handling for him.

"I've been thinking we might try some experimental video stuff," she heard him tell Steve. "We can use the studios of Southwest Pix, although naturally if we plan to branch out into the field, we'll develop facilities of our own." And one day to Buffie: "Would you check on the copyright for *After Hours*, Buffie? We've had an offer from a decaffeinated coffee to use it in a commercial. And while you're at it, I'm thinking of putting together some of our old stuff—here's a tentative list. I want to make up one of those mail-order record packages. We could advertise it on television. We ought to be getting in on that market, and I think there's still mileage in those old songs."

Often he looked in on Lee.

"How are plans for the reception coming?"

"Fine. I've completed a preliminary guest list. I'll hand it over to Buffie. She can probably add to it."

"Decorating, flowers, you're seeing to that?"

"Yes, of course."

An hour later he appeared once more in her doorway, a sheaf of papers in his hand. Her eye caught on the long fingers, tanned and supple, and her heart did an odd turnover.

"Did I mention a band?" he asked. "We'll want a band, of course."

She dragged her gaze away from his hands and with some difficulty concentrated on what he was saying.

"A band? Yes, I'm sure I can get the Mother Lode."

"The what?" His blue eyes widened.

"The Mother Lode. They're a very good local country band. I think that would be suitable, don't you?"

He smiled disarmingly. "I'll leave that up to you. If you think they're right, I'm sure they are." He started to leave, then turned back to her. "Where did you grow up?" he asked suddenly.

Once again taken by surprise by one of his lightning-quick subject changes, Lee stammered, "Where did I what?"

"Grow up."

"Right here. Not Dallas exactly, but a few miles away. On the other side of Lake Ray Hubbard. A small ranch that Dub owned. Dub's sister kept house for us after Mama died."

"Is it still there?"

"Yes, and Aunt Bess too."

Once when she was on the telephone, he waited for her to finish. Out of the corner of her eye she saw him looking at the big picture of her father, studying it curiously. When she had hung up, he asked with a quizzical look that crinkled up his eyes in the way she had noticed before, "Did you always call your father Dub?"

"Ever since I can remember. I suppose because Aunt Bess did. Some people called him W.W., but then I guess it was inevitable that it would get shortened."

He nodded as if he were considering it. She noticed that every bit of information that came his way was filed away in its proper place. Nothing seemed too insignificant to him. Everything deserved his attention or at least his consideration.

"Ever miss it?" he asked unexpectedly one day.

"Miss what?"

"That ranch you grew up on."

"Oh. Goodness, I don't know. Well—yes, sometimes I do miss it, I guess."

Next time he stopped in, she was ready for him.

"Where did *you* grow up?" she asked before he could speak.

His expression was surprised at first. Then he grinned.

"Lake Forest."

For a brief moment the thought flashed through Lee's mind that the wealthy Chicago suburb—the "Gold Coast"—where Ben Cameron grew up must be a far cry from the windswept ranch where she ran and played as a little girl.

"Ever miss it?" she teased.

"Never," he said firmly, and they both laughed.

Curiously, it was the laughing that bothered her after he had left. She disliked the fact that he seemed to be taking her in, winning her over as he had won Buffie and Steve. All the dynamic Cameron charm, she felt sure, was being turned on to make her more readily accept the changes he was planning to bring about in the company. Not that she could do anything to stop them anyway, of course, but an office staff furthering his new schemes would be much easier for him to work with than a staff which might question and raise objections. He had sensed her animosity from that very first day. He was working on it systematically, breaking it down bit by bit. It made her cross with herself to think she could be so easily taken in. Even more, she felt a strange reaction toward him, a reaction that surprised and confused her. A tingling awareness, a throbbing response in her own body, a thing beyond her control. She was physically attracted to Ben Cameron. She had to admit it to herself. She might be attracted, she thought angrily, but that was as far as it would go. There was no way she would ever reveal her feelings outwardly so that he might notice. What he saw in her was someone who could help him in business. People were tools to businessmen like the Cameron brothers. Her long experience in the music field was something that was helping him to learn. Once he had mastered it himself, he would no longer need her.

Still, there was little time for reflection. Arrangements for the Garrett-North reception were taking all her attention. And in any case, Lee thought ruefully, what's the point of digging my heels in, arguing and worrying? I've been given a raise and a fancy title. Why not sit back and enjoy the benefits as Buffie advises? But even as she offered herself this logical argument, a small voice far back in her head answered her. Because this was Dub's company and then mine, and because it means more to me than anything in the world. And because I can't bear to see some millionaire with cost-efficient schemes turn it into a shiny, empty thing with profit as its only motive. She could hear Ben Cameron's smooth argument. *Yes, I suppose I do plan to change it—in the direction of showing a profit. Any objections to that?*

What objections could she possibly raise?

On Thursday of that first week she spent a good part of her time out of the office, consulting with the band she had hired for the reception, deciding with them what sort of music would best suit the gathering and asking them to be sure to include a generous sprinkling of Dub's most popular songs. Then she met with the florist, remembering at the last minute that flowers should also be sent to Nikki North's suite in the San Carlos Hotel. She had already talked to the hotel kitchen about the food, and the invitations were ready for the mail. Short notice, but no one would object to that, she guessed, in view of all the glitter and importance attached to the affair.

It was midafternoon by the time she returned to the office, spent and tired, her makeup worn away, her turquoise blouse sticking to her back, white skirt a wrinkled mess. She was feeling irritable and decidedly unglamorous. She pushed open the door to WW Music, to be confronted by a blond beauty of twenty or so sitting behind a long shiny desk that had been drawn up at right angles to the front entrance. Behind her, painters had already set up ladders and distributed drop cloths, so that the dazzling beauty at the door was all the more striking in her perfect makeup and immaculate pink knit dress. She gave Lee a politely curious look which did not quite disguise the first reaction of critical inspection that had crossed her face when Lee entered. Lee could see her eyes taking in every bedraggled detail from unkempt hair on down.

The girl's eyes went to the bulging folder she was carrying, then, Lee could tell, to her general look of dishevelment.

"Yes?" the girl said coolly. "May I help you?"

Lee could only stare. "May I ask who—" she began.

The girl interrupted crisply, "Are those the carpet samples? Mr. Cameron would like to inspect them personally, but I believe he's busy at the moment. If you'll wait here . . ."

Lee had just opened her mouth to reply when a voice called out authoritatively behind the receptionist, "It's all right, Jennifer. I don't believe you've met Miss Colder, our senior vice president."

The girl's color changed as her face became suffused with an embarrassed flush. Lee, who had been cross and irritated and about to rebuke her sharply, was all at once sorry for her. Ben Cameron, coming out of his own office, wore a look of amusement that caused the corners of his mouth to twitch uncertainly as he tried to hold it back. His eyes danced with mirth even as his expression struggled to remain sober. "Jennifer is our new receptionist, Lee. Buffie hired her earlier today."

"I'm so sorry, Miss Colder," the girl stammered. "I didn't realize. . . ."

Lee plopped the heavy folder down on the big new desk and let out a weary sigh. "It's perfectly all right, Jennifer," she said. "Glad to have you with us." All of a sudden she felt like laughing, but she held it in for fear of adding to Jennifer's obvious distress. Then, raising her eyes again to Ben Cameron's, she felt all the amusement drain away from her. The scene had obviously entertained him, just as her own appearance must have. She was all at once acutely aware of how she looked, how bedraggled beside the perfection of the beautiful Jennifer. And where a moment before she had held in laughter, now suddenly she could feel tears welling up behind her eyes and catching at her throat.

"Quite a hectic day," she managed to stammer, and picking up her folder, she marched past both of them toward her own office. A painter's ladder had been set up just outside the door, however, and a wrinkle of tarpaulin caught her foot and made her trip just as she ducked under the ladder. She recovered her balance, slammed the folder down on her own desk and marched to the window to look out and recover her composure.

"Take the rest of the day off, Lee," said a voice from the doorway a moment later. She turned and saw him standing just inside it, looking cool and poised and casual in his dark slacks and the white shirt open at the throat and contrasting so vividly with tanned skin. "You've been working harder than any of us. You're worn out."

"I'm perfectly all right," she snapped, but admitting to herself that what made her angriest was the knowledge that she probably *looked* worn out.

"And take tomorrow off while you're at it."

"Oh really, that's not necessary. I still have a lot to do."

"Nothing that won't keep. I know for a fact how well you've organized all the plans for this thing next week. Forget it for a day. The painters will be all over the place tomorrow anyway."

"They won't bother me. There's plenty I can do."

He crossed the room in long strides and put both hands on her shoulders. "Hey, Lee, no more of that now. This company needs you. Don't start wearing yourself out. Take a little time off. Enjoy a rest."

The hands that gripped her shoulders were strong and lean. Lee could feel that strength all the way through skin and muscle, down to the very bone, it seemed. Heat which had nothing to do with the heat of the day was penetrating her too, body and being, reaching every part of her, sending her blood racing wildly. Absurdly she felt herself beginning to tremble. She tried to control it, but it seemed beyond her, a thing stronger than her will.

As though sensing the struggle in her, he tightened his grip on her shoulders and pulled her to him, enclosing her firmly in his arms and then with one hand tipping her face up to his. For a startled moment Lee's breath caught in a gasp of response as his lips came down to meet hers in a kiss of infinite tenderness which, in the long moment she clung to him, changed to one of growing passion and sensuality. Lee could feel her trembling stop and her own senses warm to a responsive passion that matched his own. Then suddenly his words echoed unexpectedly in her head. *This company needs you.* But of course! The company needed her. And the company didn't care what she looked like or whether her panty hose had a run or her makeup had worn away. But the company did worry that she might wear herself out and not be able to function. Oh yes, the company certainly worried about that! And so all this concern, this flattering attention, was really concern over an important piece of property, or more aptly, machinery. Keep it operating, oil it up, and be sure to give it a rest every now and then. Don't wear it out as long as it still has its uses.

She wrenched herself away from him. "I'm fine," she said in a calm, icy voice. "Please don't worry about me. I've never been the sort to collapse in a crisis."

"I never for a moment thought that you would." His face grew serious. The blue eyes which had shot sparks of amusement in the outer office, which had flamed with intimacy only a moment ago, bored into her now, penetrating and sharp. "It was you I was worried about."

"There's no need for that," she shot back. "I assure you I'm not the type to have a nervous breakdown over a little extra work."

She could see a sudden movement in his lean cheek as if he had clenched his jaw. "If you say so," he said coldly, raking her with a frosty look. "However, I do want you to feel free to come and go as you like—certainly until we're out of this mess in the office."

"Thank you," she snapped.

She saw the movement again, a sudden flick of muscle at the corner of his mouth, anger held in.

"Suit yourself," he said, and for a moment Lee thought a curtain had been pulled aside, allowing her a glimpse of that other Ben Cameron whose existence she had suspected. But the moment passed; his face was once again a mask, correct and unemotional. It was, she thought, the face of a man who never lost control of his emotions for long, and even more, who never lost sight of his goals.

He smiled, a small, tight smile that did not reach the icy blue of his eyes. "I'd like you to feel that you're your own boss, Lee."

She stood there looking up at him and said slowly and with ironic emphasis, "It doesn't do any harm to pretend, I suppose."

He seemed to be contemplating a reply, but then he gave a brief nod instead and turned away from her, ducking so that his tall frame would miss the ladder as he left. Lee stood for a few minutes more at the window, looking out over the sun-washed Dallas street with its hum of busy afternoon traffic. Then, making a sudden decision, she turned and left the office, hurrying past the new receptionist's desk with the briefest of nods.

She had left her car at the curb down the street from the office. Now as she got in and turned the key, she could feel the heat and stuffiness of the day returning. Texas was at its best in April, but its strong Southwestern sun was already showing its power. She flipped on the air-conditioning in the ten-year-old BMW that had been Dub Colder's and heard its reassuring hum. She drove to the corner and pulled up for a red light. Feeling again the rocketing impact of his lips pressing hers, she experienced a strange, hot surge throughout her body which she could not seem to control. When the light turned green, she made a quick, impulsive decision. Instead of turning right toward her apartment and a cool evening at home—barefooted, enjoying a tall glass of iced tea and the new novel she had just started—she turned left toward Loop 635 and the elegant new Galleria shopping mall.

The Galleria was a multilevel structure with all the floors open to an ice-skating rink on the bottom level. Coming in out of the heat of the day to its welcome coolness, to the sight of the skaters incongruously, on such a day, enjoying the ice, Lee felt herself beginning to unwind. Realizing that she had not stopped to eat all day, she bypassed the inexpensive fast-food restaurants on the first level and let the escalator carry her to the topmost floor where a quieter, more exclusive restaurant overlooked the rink from a dramatic height. She was shown to a table where she sat for a time enjoying coffee and tiny sandwiches which, along with the subdued elegance of the place, began to make her feel relaxed, pampered, and a million miles away from the unreality of that passionate moment in her office. She began to feel glad she had come here, almost able to convince herself that the moment had never truly happened. When, after eating, she went to the smartly furnished ladies'

room to touch up her makeup and hair, she studied her own
reflection critically and then, after a moment, turned with the
abruptness of her decision and left the restaurant. For a time
she walked up and down the attractive promenades, passing
by beckoning windows displaying the latest in fashions, jewelry, shoes, gourmet foods. Saks, Marshall Field, Gump's, all
tempted her, but for the moment she was content merely to
browse, inspect, absorb. Then in front of a small, exclusive
boutique with an artfully decorated window, Lee paused,
lingered, and finally went inside.

Madness, she thought. Utter madness. She swung the wheel
of the venerable BMW expertly as she made her way through
the traffic on her way east toward her own apartment complex. She was as conscious of the packages on the back seat as if
they had been extra passengers. Whatever had gotten into
her, indulging herself so shamelessly, making such ruinous
inroads on her checking account? Knowing, but still ashamed,
she bit her lower lip as she admitted to her secret, critical self
that she wanted Ben Cameron to see her in something other
than denim and boots or sensible office clothes. The hardwork-
ing Lee Colder who crawled under desks, whose shirt fre-
quently pulled out of its waistband, whose hair invariably flew
in every direction, and who was taken as a carpet saleslady by
beautiful receptionists, might be valuable to the company, but
compared to the svelte, sophisticated women of Ben Cameron's world, she was hardly worthy of notice; certainly she
would never rate a second look. And why did she want a
second look from him anyway? But no matter how she tried to
forget it, the memory would not go away—the feel of those
strong hands that had gripped her shoulders, the mouth that
had pressed against hers so hungrily. He was only trying to
placate me, her sensible mind insisted. Only flattering me in a
way he must have done often before with women. But small,
flickering flames still darted along her arms when she relived it
even now, hours later.

A horn prodded her from somewhere in back of her and she

realized the traffic light in front of her had turned green. She shifted gears and moved ahead, but the feeling was growing in her with every passing second that she had done a foolish thing, and that her rashness would lead to pain and regret.

CHAPTER FOUR

Lee's habit of rising early was so deeply ingrained that she had long since given up the use of an alarm clock, but the next morning, for the first time since she could remember, she overslept. When she saw it was nearly eight o'clock, she bounced out of bed and headed toward the shower, all in one motion, scolding herself every step of the way.

"Of all the times I didn't want to be late!" she reminded herself as she soaped and rinsed under the pounding water. Perversely she admitted that it was precisely because Ben Cameron had told her to take the day off that she was determined not to—wanted, moreover, to be on the job and at her desk early as if to rebuke him, to show him that she needed no special consideration. She shampooed her hair under the shower, towel-dried it, and then slipped into her terry-cloth robe and picked up the blow dryer. Brushing and drying, seeing her hair pick up burnished lights, she began to feel some of yesterday's emotions leave her. An optimism that had never entirely deserted her, even in the bad times, seemed to be welling up inside her. A legacy from Dub, perhaps, she thought, who could sing one moment of those bad times and in the next start tapping his booted foot to an up-tempo song that held all the joy and promise of living. And sometimes both sadness and joy were in one song. His biggest hit, "One More Heartache," was like that. Under her breath Lee started to sing it, "One more heartache doesn't matter, I still love you . . ." The hair dryer hummed, her voice rose. She sang as she had sung it so often with him—Dub carrying the melody, her voice coming in true and sweet with harmony over the top.

"The shadows on my heart I'm rearranging, to start again and give love one more try . . ."

Now another sound was intruding, persistent and repeated, nudging its way in over the low roar of the dryer and the sound of her own voice. She had left the bathroom door open and the noise was coming through with annoying intensity. She pushed the hair dryer's Off button and listened. It was the buzzer at her door being pressed, released, then pressed again.

Lee put down the dryer, frowning at an interruption on a day when she was especially anxious to hurry. She yanked the tie of her robe tighter around her waist and went to answer. Her breath caught in a gasp as she flung the door open.

"I didn't know you sang," Ben Cameron said pleasantly. He was standing there, one hand raised to lean against the doorframe as if he had been waiting for some time. "That's how I knew you were home. I heard you." His long, slow look was taking in the red-gold hair that tumbled over her shoulders, the deep parting of the white robe that showed the swell of her breasts, still moist and dewy from her shower.

"I don't," she stammered. "Not really—that is, only in the shower. Or sometimes when I'm cooking."

He was still lounging in the doorway, casually dressed, she noticed, in a short-sleeved knit shirt and tan slacks.

"May I come in?"

"Oh yes, of course." She let go of the doorknob as though it were hot and stepped back quickly. He came in and closed the door behind him. "There were a couple of things I wanted to discuss with you."

Her hand came up to hold the robe more tightly together in front. He took note of the gesture and seemed amused.

"Oh really?" she said. "Wouldn't they have waited? I mean, I'll be in the office in half an hour or so."

"That's what I thought," he grinned. "I figured you wouldn't do it."

"Do what?"

"Take the day off. I told you to, remember?"

She remembered. But more, she remembered what had followed. That sudden embrace, his mouth covering hers in a kiss that had seemed to consume her very soul with its heat. This morning he was as casual as any chance acquaintance, all passion put aside—or forgotten. She was determined to match his offhand mood, to show quite clearly that it had meant as little to her as to him. For that was obviously how he felt about it.

"Goodness, I have lots to do," she said briskly. "I couldn't possibly—"

"Do you know how many times I've heard you say that in the few days I've been here?" His eyes were still riveted on her with an intensity that made her feel totally undressed. She could not help recalling how she had clung to him the day before, and her blood went rushing wildly in spite of her best efforts to act indifferent. She pulled her composure firmly around her like her robe.

"It's not something you should complain about, coming from an employee, is it?" she asked tartly.

"No, you're right, it isn't. Even so, today I decided to do something about it," he said easily.

In spite of herself, Lee was beginning to feel warmth creeping upward from her very toes, a tremulous, unfamiliar warmth. Trying to ignore it, she asked, "What is it you've decided to do?"

"Take the day off. You and I will take the day off together."

For the first time she began to understand his casual outfit. Still, she could not help protesting, "Oh goodness, I couldn't possibly. I have so much—" She stopped short, looking up at him, and they both laughed. "Well, I do," she protested. "Besides, Buffie will wonder what's happened to me."

He shook his head. "Nope, no escape there, I'm afraid. I told her yesterday before I left the office what I was planning. She seemed to think it was a fine idea. And you know perfectly well she can hold things down in the office, with Steve to help her. Besides, don't forget there's Jennifer now to field the phone calls and visitors. She's pretty good at holding off nuisance callers."

"So I notice," Lee said, and they both laughed again. She was beginning to feel more comfortable with him, but underneath there was an uneasiness that remained. Part of it had to do with that strange, searing kiss and her own response to it, but another part was left over from her impression that first day that there was more to Ben Cameron than the suave facade indicated.

"Besides," he said, "this isn't something I'm doing for you. It's something you're going to do for me."

"How do you mean?"

"You're going to take me sightseeing. I've hardly seen anything since I landed at Love Field. Just my condo and the office. Besides, Buffie's hiring a secretary for me today. I don't want to be involved—rather leave it up to her, since I trust her judgment. So what should an outlander from Chicago see around here? What's first?"

She smiled, feeling her guarded animosity melt away as she heard his derogatory description of himself as an outlander. Someone who commanded an empire of millions, private planes, luxurious hotel suites, someone who had only to pick up the telephone to order the world and its wonders to appear at his door.

"Well, it's April," she said. "In Texas that means bluebonnets. We should certainly go somewhere and appreciate them first."

"Bluebonnets," he echoed. "I suppose I should have known you'd think of something like that." His eyes, which had not left her since he entered the apartment, seemed to have softened, but their intensity had, if anything, increased, so that now they appeared to be probing deep inside her. Nervously she said, "When I was little, I was always disappointed that I didn't have eyes the color of bluebonnets."

He said in a low voice, "I can't imagine how that would have been an improvement."

She said nothing, but stood there returning his look, not

quite aware that she was doing so. After a moment he said lightly, "That's an absolutely fetching outfit, and I really can't see how it could be improved upon either, but do you think it's quite the thing for a day of sightseeing?"

"Oh—I'm sorry," Lee stammered. Her hand had fallen away from the neck of her robe, leaving it more open than before, and once again she clutched it together. "I'll just be a minute. Please sit down." She gestured with her free hand. "Anywhere. Just make yourself comfortable." She saw his eyes go around the small, cozy apartment with its simple furniture, bookcases, plants. Then she turned and fled to the bedroom.

Once inside it, she closed the door and leaned against it, trying to catch her breath. What am I letting myself in for? she thought wildly. For a moment she had the uneasy feeling that today would prove to be, for her, a costly mistake, that after today nothing would be the same. She feared that she would be, in some way she could not anticipate now, over her head, in deep water and sinking. She lifted her head slowly and saw in the mirror on the opposite wall a slender girl with flyaway red-gold hair and green eyes looking back at her. Lee took a deep breath, stood up straight, and crossed the room to the closet where three new outfits had hung since the day before.

"Which way first?" he asked, and looked down at her, sitting beside him on the seat of the long, low Lincoln. She had chosen to wear a vivid green blouse that highlighted her eyes and hair, along with a pale yellow skirt and slim, bare sandals. She had seen the surprise and admiration in his eyes when he saw her in the outfit. But now, outdoors in daylight and headed into the day's busy traffic, Lee began to forget the misgivings she had had earlier, the sense of significance she had had about the day. It was merely a day like any other, she told herself sensibly, and she had been foolishly dramatic to embroider anything more around it. She made up her mind that she would keep the tone of things light.

"To the corner where the light is and turn left," she ordered. "We might as well start with the Cotton Bowl."

"By all means," he grinned.

Lee acted as tour guide along the way, pointing out land-marks as he wove skillfully in and out of traffic. She made a special effort to avoid looking at the long tanned fingers that held the steering wheel for fear she would remember too vividly how they had felt gripping her shoulders.

"This southeastern end of Dallas is not particularly elegant," she admitted, "but in addition to the Cotton Bowl, it also has Fair Park, where the big state fair is held each year. So of course you have to see it."

"Of course," he agreed as they drove past it. "Now continue east?"

"Yes. We'll head out of the city and I'll show you Lake Ray Hubbard."

"Now *that* sounds like a real point of interest."

"You want to see bluebonnets, don't you?" she demanded with mock sternness.

"Ah, by all means."

The lake was at the eastern edge of the city. Its banks, recently developed with luxury condominiums, rose steeply from the water. Bluebonnets grew over the slopes in thick, lavish profusion. Even though the day was bright and warm, a wind was whipping the water, causing small bass boats to bob and dip.

"Quite spectacular," he said.

"But this is nothing, really. Not compared to the hill coun-try."

"One doesn't think of Texas as having hills."

"Oh, it does. And the wildflowers there are—oh, just inde-scribable. Tourists come flocking to Austin every year just to see them."

He made no comment, and she glanced at him, thinking he was holding something in, some comment or a smile.

"I know Texans do everything on a grand scale," he said at last, "but is this considered—you know, a large lake?"

"Well, yes, around here we consider it large." She studied his face for a moment, watching it break into a broad grin, and then suddenly realized what was amusing him. "Lake Michigan," she said, remembering where he had grown up. "All right, that's one for your side. I suppose it would look like an ocean beside this."

"What about that ranch where you grew up?" he asked.

She pointed. "Over in Sulphur Springs, about a hundred miles further east."

"I thought you said outside of Dallas."

"Only a hundred miles," she said teasingly. "Around here we don't consider that any distance at all."

"Okay, score one for *your* side." They both laughed, and he followed her directions for turning back onto the westbound highway. "What next?"

Lee thought about it. She was beginning to feel more at ease with him, even though she was still acutely aware of his strong physical presence.

"Let's head west now, only go right through the city instead of around it, so you can see some of the residential streets."

"Lead on, Captain," he said.

They spent the better part of the morning driving up and down streets lined with oak and pecan trees, Lee acting her part of guide. "Swiss Avenue," she explained. "These are original Dallas mansions, now restored. . . . And this is Bryan Avenue, runs parallel to Swiss . . . careful up ahead, these four lanes are going to become two . . . the trees on both sides are very old. . . ."

Once they passed a white brick house standing back from the street behind wrought-iron fencing. Three cars were parked in the driveway, a Rolls-Royce, a DeLorean, and a Jaguar. As though sensing Lee's sudden quiet, he asked, "Is that house special in some way?"

She did not look at him. "In a small way perhaps. I used to live there."

It flooded back over her, the memory of those days and of the whole feast-or-famine way of living that had been Dub's. The house had been bought the year "One More Heartache" hit the top of the country charts and the pop charts as well.

Only eighteen months later she had found herself back on the ranch in Sulphur Springs. She explained it to him briefly.

"I see," he said softly. He drove on and for a time did not attempt further conversation. Then at last, upon reaching an intersection, he said, "Now which way? Bearing in mind that I'm starving."

"So am I," she confessed with a laugh. "Suppose we turn right then, and head for North Dallas. There's a small lake there. And no more comparisons, please—I admit this one is small. But there's a nice restaurant overlooking it. Do you like Greek food?"

"Grape leaves, eggplant, lamb—just lead me to it."

"Do you know, I just realized I skipped breakfast?" she said.

They lingered over lunch, watching the play of light and color on the water, talking now and then but not making a conscious effort to keep conversation going. Both of them were willing to enjoy the silences as well, for oddly, the silences were not awkward. Silver clinked on dishes all around them. Waiters moved discreetly in and out among the well-dressed luncheon crowd.

Refilling her cup with hot coffee from the silver pot on the table, he asked suddenly, "Do you ever miss the house on—what was it?—Park Lane?"

She glanced at him, thinking how he was always surprising her with the unexpected way his mind worked.

"No, never," she replied, shaking her head. "I was glad to go back to the ranch. I tried to tell Dub that, but I'm not sure he believed me."

"I'm not sure I would have either," he smiled at her. "Most women wouldn't give up that kind of life easily."

"I was still young then—"

"But already a woman, I should imagine, in all the ways that count."

"No, I missed the ranch, the horses. I liked the country. I never did like a lot of—things—around me."

"Oh come on now."

"Is that so hard to believe?" she asked quizzically.

"Well, if it's true, you're certainly the first woman I ever knew who—" He paused, leaving Lee to wonder what kind of women he had known.

"I think possessions, luxuries, become burdens after a time," she said thoughtfully. "I tried to tell Dub that, and I think eventually he believed me, because you see, that's the way he was too. Only he was doing it for me. He felt I should have more. He was away so much, and I was little when my mother died. He wanted to give me things. That was in the beginning when he was making a lot of money. But I was glad when he got rid of the house. He wanted by that time to invest everything in the company, and I didn't care. It wasn't my kind of life ever."

Both of them drank their coffee in silence. Then, studying her across the table, he said curiously. "You went through bad times as well as good, obviously. It couldn't have been easy always. And your father's fortunes did go downhill badly— well, I'm only saying what we both know, so don't get angry with me for putting it into words." He added this quickly as he saw her eyes flash a warning signal. "Yet you never complain about it. You've never said a word about Dub Colder that wasn't praise."

Stung by his words and about to make a sharp retort, Lee paused. Was he saying anything untrue, or even anything derogatory about Dub? Wasn't he merely voicing facts, the way any clear-thinking businessman would? For the first time she felt an unfamiliar longing to share her feelings about her father with someone.

"Yes, there were bad times," she said softly. "And Dub wasn't the world's greatest businessman. I've always known that. But I always felt it wasn't important. Because there was greatness in him. And greatness has to be forgiven its minor faults. Even its minor sins."

"That's very well put," he said thoughtfully. "Now tell me one more thing. What was it that made Dub Colder great?"

She frowned as she returned his look. "That's a very strange question. I'm not sure I understand what you're after."

His broad shoulders lifted slightly in a shrug.

"I'm not after anything really. Just the truth. I'm trying to understand this new business I'm in."

She said slowly, "I think it was that he never sang anything he didn't mean. Every time he sang a song, you thought, he's singing that for me. Words counted with him, not just music. It was all from his heart. And people responded to that."

She paused, thinking she had probably said it badly or inadequately, thinking there was much more that she should have said, but it seemed to satisfy him. He nodded faintly and then, with one of those abrupt changes of mood that she was beginning to expect from him, he said with a grin, "What's next on the tour?"

She laughed. "Goodness, haven't you had enough yet?"

"Not nearly. This is all part of my education."

Lee thought for a minute. "Well then, there's one more place I think you should see."

"Another scenic wonder like Lake Ray Hubbard?" he teased.

"Never mind, Tenderfoot. You'll see when we get there."

They took I-30, the main route westward to Fort Worth. He parked the car according to Lee's directions, on a side street, and then the two of them walked down Exchange Avenue toward the railroad tracks and the old cattle pens.

"The heart of the stockyard area," Lee explained to him. "Fort Worth was a cow town, you know."

"But not any more, surely."

"No, but proud of its background, and not anxious to be as modern as Dallas. A great deal of it has been restored. The old Stockyard Hotel, Cattlemen's steakhouse, the White Elephant Saloon—Dub used to sing there sometimes. Supposedly it was a stopping place for Butch Cassidy and the Sundance Kid on the way to Mexico—something of a Fort Worth legend."

It was easily ten degrees cooler in the shelter of the roofed-over stockyards. It was quiet too among the empty chutes and pens; the only sound was an eerie sighing breeze that blew through, flattening a scrap of newspaper against a rail fence. As they walked along together, not speaking, she began to feel an intense physical awareness of him, so strong that it was almost tangible. His face wore a look of concentration, as though he were imagining something, seeing it in his mind's eye. She could guess what it was.

"Can you picture it?" she asked in a low voice. "As it must have been back in the days of the big cattle drives?"

He shot her a look of surprise. "That's what I was doing. I was thinking how it must have looked then—all the pens filled, men and cattle milling around, horses, dust, heat, noise."

And he would have fit into that picture, she thought. As a tall, rangy cowboy, lean-muscled and sun-browned. He would have had the same strong qualities as now, even though the twentieth century had provided an overlay of sophistication. The powerful attraction she was feeling toward him made her suddenly weak and unsteady. She stopped by one of the pens and held tight to the railing.

"And even now it isn't entirely deserted," she said, trying to keep her voice conversational and steady. He stood beside her, arms resting on the railing, and followed her look. Inside the pen were a blanket, an empty wine bottle, a pile of newspapers. His forehead drew together in a puzzled frown.

"You mean someone's been in here? Sleeping, or what?"

She nodded. "Homeless men stay here—hoboes, I suppose you'd call them."

"But where are they now?"

She lifted a hand to point toward a darkened passageway. "The different parts of the stockyards are connected by underground tunnels. Whoever was here"—she nodded toward the blanket—"he's gone in there to hide and wait until we leave."

"You mean he heard us coming."

She nodded.

They turned and retraced their steps, speaking little until they were back in the car and headed eastward toward Dallas.

She watched the curve of his fingers as they held the wheel loosely but still with firm control, and thought, whatever happens in the future, I'm glad we had today. It means something to me even if it was only a bit of sightseeing for him.

He glanced at her briefly, his blue eyes curious and questioning. Then he looked back at the highway, maneuvering skillfully into another lane. "There was a reason why you wanted me to see that, wasn't there?"

She looked down at her hands in her lap. "Yes. Because you asked me about Dub back in the restaurant. You wanted to know what made him great. I don't think I explained it very well. But now you've seen the stockyards—well, Dub used to go there, often. Sometimes when he was appearing at the White Elephant he'd go there and spend hours between shows. And he'd sit with those men, talk with them. When *he* came, you see, they didn't hide. He was their friend—he talked their language. And he'd take his guitar and sing—not to them, but with them. Some of his greatest songs came out of those times. 'Wanderin' Man,' 'Home to Nowhere.' "

She glanced cautiously at his sharp, lean profile, wondering how much he understood of what she was saying, how much he was dismissing as merely the bias of an adoring daughter. It was several moments before he spoke again.

"I'm glad you took me there," he said.

It was late afternoon before they arrived back at the garden apartment complex where Lee lived. He parked the car and walked with her to the entrance of her building. Silence wrapped itself around them, as though the day they had shared had left them both drained. The air had grown heavy and sultry. Lee thought she could feel a change in the weather looming, and for a moment, walking along beside him, trying to match her stride to his long one, she asked herself whether the change might not be in her as much as in the air around her. Certainly her emotions were in a state of greater turmoil than when she had started out that morning. She had still felt then a bitter resentment at the way he had assumed the day before that a small attention, a casual kiss, would keep her happy and satisfied in her job. Yet today the resentment had melted away in the warmth of what seemed to be genuine friendliness on his part.

Friendliness. The word carried its own bitterness with it. For it was certainly not what she was feeling toward him. It was too mild a word to describe the surge of longing, the heat of desire that swept through her when she found herself this close to him. But she knew it to be a dangerous attraction and one-sided—entirely on her part. And what was the matter with her anyway, allowing herself to give in to it? Was it perhaps his sympathetic attention, all those questions he had asked—his apparently genuine interest in her? Whatever the cause, it was a thing to be guarded against, and she knew it.

She cast a quick, upward look at his face as they stood before her door and felt a stab of surprise as she saw that he was studying her, blue eyes bright and probing.

"I hate to have today end," he said suddenly. "Why don't we have dinner together?"

Something turned over inside Lee, something warm and throbbing and shot through with a sudden flash of hope, as bright as the lightning that sometimes tore through the clouds on a day like this, but as quickly gone. At once she shrank back from what it implied. It would be only a casual thing for him, but it could turn out to be painful for her. Sightseeing, driving around Dallas with him was one thing, but an intimate dinner which might promote intimate topics was another altogether.

She fumbled in her handbag for her key. "It's been quite a long day," she murmured, looking down, avoiding the scalpel-sharp probing of his eyes. "I think we'd better call it quits before I collapse."

"You don't look near collapse to me," he said softly, and she could hear the smile in his voice. "Are you sure I can't change your mind?"

It took all her willpower, but she said firmly, "No, thank you. Perhaps another time."

"I'm very grateful for the tour. It's the best time I've had in Texas."

"I'm so glad if you enjoyed it." She managed to raise her head and return his look, in control of herself once more. "See you Monday in the office then," she said briskly, unlocking the door hurriedly and slipping inside.

By the time she had changed into a loose white housecoat, she could hear the wind that had started up. Instead of turning on the air-conditioning she went from window to window, throwing them open to let the fresh air blow through the apartment and dispel the day's stuffiness. She breathed in deeply, trying to clear her mind as well, trying to rid it of all the conflicting emotions that the day had produced in her. She watched the drapes blow inward, watched the mesquite trees in the courtyard move and riffle as the storm drew nearer. Yet her own restlessness stayed with her as she walked barefooted from room to room in the small apartment, arms crossed in front of her, hugging her elbows, watching the darkening skies and listening to the occasional distant thunder. Her thoughts kept her company, moving in the same restless way but always coming back to the same starting point. Worlds of difference lay between her and Ben Cameron. Differences in background, in attitudes, in experience. The women he had known, women he must have been involved with, had to have been women of sophistication who were able to meet him on a common ground and relate to him because of the similarity of their lives.

Lee walked aimlessly into her compact kitchen and thought briefly about food. But nothing appealed to her, and she returned to the living room and stood for a moment by the window, the thin white housecoat pressed against her body by the wind and its welcome coolness. It was not that she was naive, inexperienced, she told herself. She was twenty-six years old; she had had plenty of men friends; one or two of them she had loved—or thought she did, for a time. Always she had been the one to break it off, knowing that it had not been right. Her own demanding work schedule had been a thing most men did not appreciate either, she realized. Yet certainly no one could be as deeply involved in the volatile world of the music business with all its artistry and emotionalism as she had been the last few years and still remain wide-eyed and credulous. She was at least as knowing and worldly as other women—probably more so. What really loomed as a barrier between her and Ben Cameron was—there it was again—their essential difference. They were two strangers who had met in circumstances which had thrown them together, but they remained strangers—she did not fool herself about that. And being thrown together daily had nothing to do with love. It was not even to be mistaken for attraction, if one were to be honest about it. She suspected it was more curiosity than anything else, at least on Ben's part. What she herself felt —Lee turned away from the window impatiently and went on with her pacing—whatever it was, this curious stirring that she had not put a name to yet, she would handle it. It would remain her own secret too, for there was no one she felt the need to share it with, no one to answer to. Sooner or later it would play itself out just as others had in the past. One day she would wake up and find it gone. Her lips moved in a small, wry smile as she lectured herself. A few sleepless nights won't kill you, Lee Colder. When it's over, you'll be the same person you were before. That's how it's always been; you've managed on your own, you can do it again. Yet even as she repeated the words to herself, it seemed to Lee that a small inner voice argued with her, stubbornly and tenaciously, from some far corner of her mind. This time it's different, the voice insisted. This one isn't like the others. When it's over, you won't be the same. Not this time. Try as she might to shut the voice out, Lee could still hear it.

Leaving the windows open, the breeze still gusting through with its blissful coolness, she picked up the book she had been meaning to get to, turned on a reading lamp, and settled down at one end of the couch. But the ragged edges of memory, all the scenes from the day they had spent together, refused to leave her, kept tugging at her awareness, and would not let her attention fasten anywhere, even on the attractions of her favorite author. She kept looking up from the page, intensely aware of the gathering night, the approaching storm, all the sounds around her, the rustling of the trees, the silky movement of the drapes. Wearily she gave up trying to read, let the book fall from her hands, and lay there listening.

The sound of the buzzer, harsh and insistent, intruded itself violently into her consciousness. Lee's eyes flew open. The room was dark now except for the small circle of light near the lamp where she had fallen alseep. She could hear rain coming down hard. The wind, still blowing through the apartment, had gone cold and damp. Lee shivered, feeling chilled through. The buzzer sounded again. Still muddled from sleep, she felt a twinge of annoyance, guessing that it must be her neighbor, Mary Barnes. Lee had often babysat for the Barnes children, and Mary was quite apt to stop in for coffee and gossip once the children were tucked away in bed. Ordinarily Lee was glad to see her, but tonight she felt she would be poor company even for a good friend. She had no more to give, Lee thought. All her emotional reserves were, for the moment, depleted. Wearily she pulled herself up from the couch and went to open the door.

He stood there, tall and rumpled-looking, and filling the whole doorway as he had that morning. Rain spotted the shoulders of his soft knit shirt. His dark hair, damp and mussed, had fallen loosely over his forehead. In the dimness she found it difficult to read the expression on his face, but his voice was low and husky.

"Lee. . . ."

She felt disoriented, oddly unsure of herself. "Ben?" she whispered. "Did you forget something? What time is it? I must have fallen asleep."

He put a hand up slowly to touch her cheek, still warm and flushed from sleep, although her body was shivering.

"You're cold," he said tenderly, and then, "I had to come back. I had to. I kept thinking about you. I had to see you again, to hold you—" Suddenly he put his arms around her and pressed her against him so tightly that she could feel the strong outlines of his body, the trace of dampness on his shirt. He tilted her head back and sought her mouth, parting her lips with a long, hungry kiss that throbbed and beat along with her own heart. Breathless with surprise for a moment, Lee was quiet in his arms, letting feeling, sensations, longings, wash over her in a succession of pounding impulses. Then, almost without meaning to, she found herself returning his kiss, her arms coming up to press against the back of his head, to lose themselves in the thick dark hair. She heard the small inner voice cry out to her, It doesn't mean the same thing to him as it does to you, but Lee refused to listen. I know, I know, I know, she repeated in time to the insistent drumming of her own heart. I know it doesn't, but I don't care. Tonight I just don't care.

The flame that flared in both of them held an urgency that made them cling together in sudden desperate need.

"I couldn't leave you like that," he said at last, his mouth close to her hair. "I had to be with you. I had to tell you what I was feeling."

"What were you feeling?" she whispered.

"That I'd just never met anyone like you. All the way back to my apartment I kept thinking that. And when I got there I didn't even get out of the car—I just couldn't. I turned around and came back here. Then I just sat outside in the car for—I don't know for how long. Lee, I don't know what's happened to me, but whatever it is, it's driving me wild. I can't let you get away from me. I want to be with you, I want to hold you. . . ."

Lee found his lips again and drew him down to her, letting his kiss drink deeply of her own passion. Then with her mouth she traced a path down his throat to where she could feel his pulsing heartbeat.

"I'm glad you came back," she murmured, knowing suddenly what the thing had been that sent her pacing restlessly from room to room earlier. "I wanted you to." They kissed and clung together again and at last, sensing that it was all moving too fast, hurtling forward like an avalanche ready to engulf them both, Lee pulled a little away from him and smiled up at him, and he, taking his cue from her, took a deep breath and grinned at her.

"I did ask you out to dinner," he said. "The invitation's still good."

They still held each other, unwilling to let go, but standing slightly apart, tasting the wonder of the moment.

"Why don't we eat here?" she asked. "Homemade chili in the freezer—a Texas standby."

"Sounds great—if you're sure."

"I'm very sure," she said, and for a moment the words lay between them there in the dimly lit room. Then, abruptly, and with a small upward quirk of one side of his mouth, he said in mock seriousness, "Only first I think we'd better start mopping."

"Mopping? Oh lord! The windows!" For the first time Lee gave a startled look around and realized that rain was coming in every opened window. She made a dash into the bathroom and returned with two heavy bath towels. "Here, catch!" she cried, and tossed him one. They hurried around the apartment, closing windows, then kneeling to mop under them, closing drapes, turning on lights, until by the time they got up, breathless and laughing, the whole place had begun to look warm and welcoming with lamplight, closed in against the world. Lee took the two sodden towels and tossed them into the bathroom, then hurried to the kitchen and took a flameproof casserole of chili from the freezer and popped it into a low oven to warm.

"There now. That'll take a while to heat up," she said, straightening, but he was there behind her, his arms quickly circling her waist to turn her to him.

"How long?" he whispered.

"Oh—a while . . ."

"Good," he said softly as he bent to kiss her again.

The moments while they waited for the chili to be ready

were for Lee moments of pure unreality and enchantment. When she began to set the table, he was beside her, his hand moving to cover hers as she laid the napkins beside the plates. When she turned to him in surprise, he covered her mouth with his and held her close to him. When she reached for two wine glasses on a shelf above her head, his long arms reached them first, bringing the glasses down and all in the same motion folding his arms around her, kissing her hair. It was as if he could not see, feel, touch her enough to satisfy himself that she was real. Lee, responding to his nearness, felt herself going limp with longing and desire even as she told herself it was all moving too fast, hurtling toward some unseen danger up ahead. It was as if some strong yet somehow fateful influence had acted upon this particular day. Their closeness in the car, the eerie solitude of the stockyards, the threat of storm, then the thundering downpour—it was a moment, a day, plucked out of time, full of the throb of passion, heat, wonderment, yet loaded too with warnings, omens, signs of danger. I must be careful, Lee kept telling herself. I must be the one to be cautious for both of us. By Monday morning he will be sorry about it all, or if not sorry, offhand, which is worse. Because I'm new to him, he's attracted. I'm a novelty, nothing more. I must keep it in perspective. I mustn't let my heart run away with me. I mustn't let my own physical longings do the dictating. I must be the one to recognize that it's only a passing thing.

Yet even as she kept issuing sensible warnings to herself, the touch of his lips, the strength of his arms acted upon her like wine. She began to feel limp and helpless with love, trapped by a passion that she felt she had been waiting for all her life. Standing in the close circle of his arms, feeling the outlines of his body, the warmth of his hands on her skin through the thin white housecoat, Lee put her face up to his to receive his kiss, feeling all her earlier strength drain away, knowing that no matter what she had thought earlier, she had not the willpower to resist him now. Longing desperately for the touch of his body, wanting to give herself to him completely, she kissed him back feverishly, pressing his head down to hers. And it was then, in that moment of wild longing, that something sounded in her head, the words of a song that she had heard Dub sing often: "Things are going too good, baby, you're riding for a fall. . . ."

Not wanting to hear the words or their warning, she closed her eyes and gave her head a little shake, pressing her cheek against his chest and holding him still more tightly. Yet their nagging persistence would not leave her, and at last with a small sigh she put both palms flat against his chest and pulled back, looking up into his face.

"That chili must be ready by now," she whispered, and heard a small sigh escaping him, a faint groan that was an echo of her own feelings. Even so, she was relieved when they sat down to eat and could give their attention to something beyond their own yearning bodies, the intoxicating nearness of each other.

He poured the wine, commenting with a smile, "Are you sure this is right to go with chili? Shouldn't it be Lone Star in long-necks?"

She laughed at him. "Good heavens, how does a city hick know about Lone Star beer and long-neck bottles?" she teased. "That's pure Texas."

"I'm not entirely ignorant," he grinned. And then, after his first taste of the chili, with her looking at him slyly to catch his reaction: "Delicious! A masterpiece."

"Not too hot for you?"

"Certainly not. You *are* a lady of many talents."

"Not really."

"Well, I don't mind admitting I'm depending on you a lot."

She smiled across the little table at him. "Then you're leaning on a slender reed, as my Aunt Bess would say."

"Not at all. You know more than most in this business. And by the way, I'm anxious for you to see the new studios. I'd planned to take you on a tour of the place before this—only today was more fun," he added with the quick smile that made her heart turn over. "Anyway, Monday will be time enough."

"Monday?"

"That's when Nikki and Joe Bud arrive from Nashville, and I figured we'd have the contract-signing ceremony in the new studio. We'll have some of the press in for pictures and so on."

Lee could feel a chilly dread stealing over her at the thought. "Goodness, you don't need me for that, do you? I mean, Steve's the one who's good with the press. Buffie and I can hold down the fort back at the office."

"I'd like you to be there, Lee," he said. His voice was even and pleasant, but a note of firmness had crept in. Sensing it, Lee felt a small knot of stubbornness forming in herself.

"The studio's your creation," she said. "I have nothing to do with it."

"It's where we'll be doing our recording from now on—you should certainly get to know it. You should become acquainted with all the facets of our new operation. These studios were built to our specifications by a firm which specializes in such construction. I think they were one of the convincing arguments in winning over North and Garrett to come with us. Engineering has become a major factor in recording nowadays."

"I know that, of course—"

"I'm no expert, I'll admit, although I *am* learning. And I want you to meet Ed Farraday. He's our chief engineer, very knowledgeable in the field. He's supervising everything for us."

Lee made an effort to sound interested.

"Are the studios actually done? Ready for use?"

"Just about. A few finishing touches, that's all. And of course I want you to look in on where our new offices will be. Although they won't be ready for another six months or so. I felt priority should be given to the studio—"

"Offices!" Lee stared at him in astonishment. "You mean our offices are to be moved?"

"Yes, of course. I thought you understood that. WW Music, the whole Cambro complex in fact, will be in this new central location—everything together."

"But then why—I mean, all the elaborate redecorating

you're doing—all those carpets and fixing everything up. . . ."

"Just a few cans of paint and some touches here and there," he said lightly, refilling her wineglass and then his own. "After all, we'll be there for a few months. We want to be comfortable during that time and create the right impression too."

"Oh, by all means," she said, and she heard the iciness creeping into her own voice. "We certainly couldn't have stood it the way it was—not for six months."

"I didn't mean that, Lee."

"And of course you want North and Garrett to have a good impression of us." She realized she was being unreasonable, but once again she was feeling overwhelmed by the Cameron wealth and the totally different standard of values that such wealth brought with it. The idea of such an expenditure for a temporary convenience was mind-boggling to her after the penny-pinching economy measures she had been obliged to observe for the last five years. Also, she could not help feeling a pang of regret at the realization that Dub's old offices were to be abandoned.

"It's not the way you're making it sound," he argued. "It's just a good investment, that's all." For a moment he gave his attention to his plate, but she sensed that he had begun to lose interest in food. Longing to reach out and touch the disheveled lock of hair, still damp from rain, that hung across his forehead, she held back, suddenly aware that the distance between them was growing. Seconds later his fork went clattering against his plate as he dropped it and got up, all in one motion, pushing his chair back roughly and striding across the room with long, restless steps.

"Darn it, Lee!" he exploded. "Why is it I can't do anything right where you're concerned? I'm bending over backward to try to be tactful about things. I know how much the company means to you. But I'll be damned if I let you wreck my plans for it just because of your sentimental hanging on to the past. I'm going to put WW Music back on its feet—you should be glad of that. Instead, you're arguing with me every step of the way!"

"Are you going to tell me again about that great track record of yours and the way you turn around failing companies?" she blazed at him, standing up herself now and confronting him furiously.

"You were certainly glad enough to sell when we made our offer!"

"I didn't realize then that you came with the deal!"

For a long moment he regarded her across the space of the small, lamplit room which had all at once lost its warmth and coziness, had become, instead, a battleground strewn with sharp and dangerous obstacles. One of his dark eyebrows moved upward and his mouth drew into a thin, cold line.

"Well, I did come with the deal," he said slowly, mocking her words. "And much as you seem to dislike it, I am the boss now. It's my company." He flung the words deliberately at her, weapons intended to wound. "So I'd appreciate it if you'd appear at the new studio on Monday as I requested. And if you could manage to put yourself out enough to be cordial to Nikki and Joe Bud, that would be greatly appreciated too." He paused briefly and then added, "Let me put that differently. I expect you to be cordial. That's an order."

He turned and strode to the door, slamming it behind him as he went out. The sound seemed to reverberate in the room for a long time afterward.

CHAPTER FIVE

Approaching Cambro Park, Lee could see a cluster of low buildings and one taller building off to the side. That must be the hotel, she guessed. As many trees as possible seemed to have been preserved by the builders; she could see that others had been freshly planted, so that the whole feeling of the place was more that of a private resort than an office complex. Buildings were screened from each other. As she pulled into the parking area of the new studio, she could see a number of cars already parked there. The press had arrived early, she thought. One or two were vans bearing the logos of local television stations, so the Minicam crews were here as well, apparently.

She approached the front entrance with misgivings and with a tense knot in her stomach that had scarcely left her all weekend. More than anything she dreaded seeing Ben Cameron again. Much as she disliked the whole idea of the two Nashville celebrities descending on Dallas like a tornado, it was some relief to her to know that she would not be obliged to confront him alone. In the general confusion of press conference, contract signing, and picture taking, it was quite unlikely that they would be thrown together intimately. She would put in an appearance, greet the two singers with what enthusiasm she could muster, then fade into the background. And in one sense there was relief in having the lines drawn clearly between them, in having their relationship spelled out once and for all. From now on she would be an employee, a business associate, nothing more. For as long as she stayed with WW Music—and that too was a subject she was giving some thought—she would be cooperative, pleasant, and helpful. She would also keep her distance. Business was what commanded his whole attention, she reminded herself. It motivated his life. Anything else was on the fringe, a momentary diversion. She must have been dreaming the other night to think for even a moment that he would have any real interest left over for her.

She found Steve waiting for her just inside the front door.

"Hey, good, you're early," he said, grabbing her elbow and leading her into the main room of the studio, where reporters were already milling around, talking with each other, adjusting cameras. A long table had been set up at one end of the place, but it looked lost in the cavernous, high-ceilinged room. As big as a handball court, Lee thought with some wonder, involuntarily comparing it with the small rented studio they had been using in Dallas—crowded and shabby and with aging equipment.

"The big attractions aren't here yet," Steve said. "You've got time for the grand tour, if you're interested. Let's go over to the control room. It's behind that glass. Ed Farraday, the engineer, can explain everything to you."

"Oh really, it's not necessary," Lee started to protest, but at that moment a lanky young man, prematurely balding, came hurrying across the floor toward them.

"Miss Colder?" he panted. "I'm Ed Farraday—sorry I wasn't at the door to greet you. Mr. Cameron said I was to show you around as soon as you got here. Of course they're due to arrive any minute, but while we're waiting, we could look around a bit."

Lee was on the point of resisting again, but then decided it was easier to go along with his enthusiasm. He seemed so genuinely proud of the place that it would have been unkind to put a damper on his efforts.

"Fine," she said with as much cheerfulness as she could manage, and while Steve drifted off to "maintain good press relations," as he put it, but actually to engage in conversation with the prettiest of the girl reporters, Lee followed Ed Farraday as he moved across the vast room, explaining and gesturing.

"This is the main studio area, of course," he said.

"It takes my breath away."

"The control room's over there. We'll head that way. This part looks big and bare, of course, but it's been scientifically planned every step of the way. These walls are of rough cedar planking, which has an excellent absorption coefficient—gives a very natural sound. The specific frequencies of absorption are determined by Helmholtz resonators, which take into account the width of the wood slats, the depth of the space behind them, and also the amount of space between the slats —very important. The wood slats vibrate sympathetically, thus absorbing any troublesome sound energy. Over there," Ed Farraday pointed toward a corner, "is the drum area. It has a special baffling built around it to absorb the lows—those from around 40 to 160 Hz. That way we won't get the second and third harmonics from the drums affecting the piano."

"I see," Lee said, trying valiantly to understand.

"We have another such area for the acoustic piano. Our aim throughout has been to create surroundings where musicians could feel comfortable."

"Yes, of course." Lee nodded and managed to look enthusiastic. Yet she was feeling totally out of her depth. Her whole life had been lived in the music business—it was what she had heard three times a day at meals and in between as well. She had watched Dub Colder sit and compose songs, picking at his guitar and humming, frowning, doing it over and over to get it right. She had watched the charts with him, learned about coaxing distributors into taking their releases, learned about copyrights and publicity. Yet here she was lost. Ed Farraday was speaking a language she did not understand. Ben Cameron expected her to learn, to share his enthusiasm for the new techniques. According to him, she was only hanging on to the past. And who could say? Lee thought wretchedly. Perhaps he was right and she was foolishly, sentimentally wrong.

"I'm anxious for you to see the control room," Ed Farraday said eagerly, breaking into her thoughts. "The ceiling height was something that had to be decided, and at first I thought fourteen feet. But then I got to thinking about it and opted for twelve."

"You're the expert," Lee smiled at him. "You should know." Even though she felt like a traveler in a strange country, she had to admit his enthusiasm was winning.

"Well, it just seemed to me the twelve-foot height would load the sound a little tighter when it came to the bass," he said modestly.

"Sounds reasonable to me," she said, hoping she sounded interested and not hopelessly stupid about the whole matter. But he was so absorbed in his own excitement about the place that she guessed he scarcely noticed her reaction.

He opened the door to the glass-walled control room and let her precede him inside, not saying anything for a moment but looking at her eagerly to see her reaction. This time Lee did not have to pretend as she stood, wide-eyed and awe-struck in spite of herself, before the great colorful control board that was the heart of the studio. The huge board with its dozens of red, green, and blue buttons lay spread out before her with two luxurious leather chairs facing it. The wood paneling of the walls was burnished to a dull glow as were the golden parquet floor and the diagonally paneled wood ceiling.

"It's simply beautiful," Lee whispered.

Ed Farraday looked pleased. "Well, Mr. Cameron said to get the best. Spend what you need, he said. So I was in a position to buy any board at all. But I myself have always liked a very simple board, and this Trident Series 80 produces a beautiful clarity of signal. The TSM is grander-looking but it's much more complex, and you do get an unavoidable noise and cross-talk factor with it . . ."

Lee smiled brightly as he went on talking, but inwardly she was feeling a sense of bewilderment that anyone could call this vast electronic marvel "simple."

". . . so many advantages, of course, with twenty-four-track recording, and this setup should really maximize all of them—" He interrupted himself with a sudden snap of his fingers and then slapped his forehead lightly with his open palm. "Darn! I forgot to check the lounge area to see if the tile men had finished. They were making a couple of last-minute touches earlier, but I want to be sure they're out of there before Miss North arrives—you'll excuse me for just a couple of minutes, Miss Colder."

"Go right ahead," she begged. "I'll just look around by myself. And please—make it Lee, won't you?"

"Okay," he grinned as he started out through a rear door to the control room. "I want to show you the rooms back here too, if we have time before they arrive—I won't be long—"

Lee waved him off good-naturedly and stood for a moment looking around the control room. Then she moved to the glass door and looked over toward the main entrance where the reporters and photographers were clustered, waiting for the arrival of the stars. A sense of excitement was beginning to ripple through the place. She glanced at her watch, then edged out into the main room, standing by a wall hung with long velour drapes. She was feeling more nervous than she liked to admit to herself, and most of her edginess was at the prospect of seeing Ben Cameron again. Singers, even famous ones, she was used to, although stars of the magnitude of these two had been something of a rarity around WW Music lately. But the strange complexity of feelings she experienced toward her new employer, all culminating in that stormy night of passion, and later, of bitterness and resentment, were something new to her. For the first time she seemed unable to manage or control her own emotions, unable to stop their wild seesawing between attraction and animosity.

The heavy drapes beside her moved suddenly with a whirring sound, and she gave a startled step backward.

"Electrically operated," said a voice, and she whirled around to see a young man in horn-rimmed glasses and jeans, his thumbs tucked into his belt. He pressed a button on the wall and the drapes returned to their original position. "They're for sound absorbency," he explained. "You see how these rear corners of the room are rounded? This one's fully covered with wood and that one on the other side with felt over Masonite."

Another engineer, Lee thought with a silent groan. She felt she had had all the electronic wonders she could take in for one day.

"Very impressive," she murmured.

"It is," the young man agreed. "And have you seen the isolation rooms in the back? There's one that's live, with reflective wall surfaces, and another one for dead sound. Then there's a kitchenette, bathroom, lounge. And of course the Jacuzzi—"

"Jacuzzi!"

"For unwinding."

"Oh."

"That control room's something, isn't it?" he said with admiration.

"It certainly is."

"A far cry from what they had only a few years back, isn't it?"

"Yes," Lee admitted. "I was thinking that myself."

"Wonder what Dub Colder would have thought of it," he said.

Lee glanced at him with surprise, but before she could comment, the young man went on, "He's always been my idol, Dub Colder. I have all his records."

"Is that so? Dub Colder was my father," Lee said, pleased in spite of herself. "I've heard him tell how years ago when he was just starting out, they recorded on a single track, with no control board at all to speak of, just a couple of knobs for volume and tone. And even later, in the sixties when he made his big hits, it was only a two-track tape, and sometimes if they needed a bit more reverb or an echo effect, they'd record in a stairwell or even the bathroom to get that hollow sound."

"No kidding." The young man smiled. "Well, of course today's equipment is much fancier, much more sensitive. I suppose they feel that makes it easier to create a hit record." He looked around thoughtfully.

"I'm not so sure about that," Lee said, frowning. "I think the talent has to come first. All the rest is just the means to an end. And even that I'm not so sure of. I just don't know . . ."

"How do you mean, Miss Colder?" he asked, his face full of youthful eagerness.

Lee explored the thought in her own mind as she answered him. "Oh, I just think that sometimes all these—gadgets—have the opposite effect from what was intended. I mean, they make perfect records all right, but often all the heart's gone out of the music. There used to be something about live musicians facing each other, seeing each other's expressions, living the music together, that helped to produce great records. Now, with all this"—she waved her hand to take in the enormous studio, the glassed-in control room—"they record on separate tape tracks. Sometimes the musicians record one day and the vocalist the next day—all the new electronic equipment permits them to do that—sometimes they never even see each other. Canned music, that's the way I think of it. And often it seems to me it comes out sounding that way too."

"I think I'm inclined to agree with you," the young man said. He seemed about to make another comment when there was a sudden general movement and a small explosion of sound from the group near the front door. She saw Steve detach himself from the others and look around anxiously. Then, spotting her, he came at a gallop across the studio floor and seized her hand.

"Come on, Lee, they're here!" For a split second he glanced at the bespectacled young man with her and looked startled, but then at once he began to drag her back with him, saying scoldingly, "We're supposed to be the official greeters, for Pete's sake, Lee."

She waved futile apologies over her shoulder in the general direction of the young man, then hurried to keep up with Steve as they approached the crowd at the door.

"Coming through, excuse us. One side, please," Steve said, edging forward until they were standing in front of the door. "Holy smokes, Lee, what were you doing, talking to—" But the rest of his question was lost as the door swung open to admit the new arrivals.

It was Ben's tall outline that she saw first, filling the whole doorway, and for the briefest of moments their eyes seemed to catch and hold, but it was so quick, so fleeting, that Lee thought later she might have imagined it. It was the girl with him on whom all the attention focused at once.

Nikki North was tiny and slender. She came well below Ben's shoulder, and it seemed to Lee that there was a vitality and magnetism about her that responded at once to the reporters and photographers. At first she shrank back as if overcome with surprise. One small hand held Ben's arm, and she pressed her body close to his as though for protection. He placed his own hand over hers in a gesture of reassurance and with the other motioned the eager reporters back.

"Suppose we get set up over there at the table—more room for everyone," he said pleasantly. "Don't go frightening my star before I've even got her signature on the contract." There was a murmur of amusement and the reporters fell back good-humoredly so that a small space was cleared.

"Ah—Lee. Glad you made it," he said easily. "Nikki, this is Lee Colder, our vice president of marketing—and pretty much everything else." Now there could be no mistaking the look he gave her. Lee saw the quirk of one eyebrow as it lifted, caught the ironic line of his mouth, its corners tucked in, all traces of warmth and intimacy missing. They were strangers once again, as remote from each other as though they had just met.

"How do you do, Miss North," Lee said pleasantly, putting her hand out. "Welcome to WW Music."

Nikki's small hand felt soft and alive in hers. Lee could not help thinking of a kitten. Then at once the singer withdrew it after a breathy hello and tucked it back under Ben's arm.

"Goodness, I didn't expect anything like this," Nikki murmured, raising large blue eyes to his face.

Not much, Lee could not help thinking bitterly as she took note of Nikki's outfit. Show-biz Western. She wore a mid-calf glittering skirt made of a golden metallic fabric. A shirt of the same fabric, tightly fitted, its yoke dangling more fringe, its neckline plunging between shapely breasts. Her blond hair tumbled in ringlets around her shoulders and a Western-style hat hung behind her head, held by its cord, making a frame for her face. Even her high-heeled Western boots were gold. Lee could see the headlines already. "WW Music Signs Its Golden Girl. . . ."

"And this is Joe Bud Garrett, Lee," Ben was saying. "Come on now, Nikki, let's lead the way. You two follow along."

Lee heard the small breathy voice murmur, "Don't you *dare* leave me, Ben, you hear? Not for *one* minute. I'll be all right if I can just hang on to you. . . ." Suddenly Lee's hand was caught in a firm, rough handclasp and she found herself looking into a weathered face that wore a broad grin.

"Well, howdy, little lady," Joe Bud Garrett said warmly. "We sure enough have heard about you."

He was less exotic-looking than Nikki North, but his aura was still that of the seasoned professional. He was only slightly taller than Lee. He wore his sandy hair long so that it curled just above the collar of his Western shirt. He was dressed in jeans and boots, and his face had, she thought, a look of experience about it, with tiny lines at the corners of his gray eyes. But the eyes themselves were quick to light up and his smile had a genuine look. He reminded Lee of musicians who had played with Dub Colder years ago. Successful he might be, she thought, but the real country look had not left him.

"I'm so happy to meet you," she said. "This is a very exciting day for all of us."

He hung on to her hand as he studied her face. "So you're Dub Colder's girl," he said, smiling at her. "Now *that* was one of the big ones. A real giant in the business."

"Thank you," Lee said simply, feeling a sudden rush of gratitude to him for saying it. "Well—look, we'd better get over there to the table. All those people are waiting for you."

He tipped his head back and laughed. "Oh, bless your heart,

little lady, they're not waiting for me. They've got the big attraction right there. Today's her day."

Lee glanced at him curiously, thinking it an oddly generous attitude for a star of Joe Bud Garrett's prominence. And it occurred to her as they followed the others across the floor toward the long table that perhaps it was because he *was* so well established that he could afford to be magnanimous.

"Well, we're real happy to have you here in Dallas," she said. "We'll try to keep you from getting homesick for Nashville."

"No danger of that," he grinned, guiding her by a touch at her elbow. "This is like coming home. I come from Fate, you know."

"Fate, Texas?" she asked in surprise. She knew the little town well—passed through it every time she drove to Sulphur Springs to visit the ranch where she grew up.

"That's the one," he said. "You know it? Got its name stuck right up there on that big old water tower?"

"Of course I do."

"Well, maybe it was my fate to come home to it. Who knows?"

"Anyway, we're all glad you did," she said.

They reached the table and pushed through the crowd of reporters around it. Ben and Nikki were standing behind it, and as Lee and Joe Bud Garrett approached, Ben pulled out a chair for Nikki and saw that she was comfortably seated. Lee smoothed her businesslike white suit with its soft navy blouse and sat further along the table. Joe Bud sat next to Nikki, and Ben, still standing, motioned for quiet and addressed the press.

"Before I let you ask Nikki any questions, I'm going to make sure this deal's sewed up," he said with a grin. He motioned toward the papers which someone—perhaps Steve—had placed in front of her on the table, and then he handed her a pen.

Nikki closed her eyes quickly and opened them as though giving herself courage. "I am just *shaking*, I'm so nervous," she said with a tremulous little laugh. "This is the most exciting day of my whole life."

She took the pen and signed at the bottom of the contract in the spot which Ben pointed to with one long, tanned finger.

It was a noticeably firm signature, Lee noticed. Not a tremor. Then she thought, That's all there is to it. It's a fact now. She felt in a curious way that her life had changed, just in that moment, that things would not be the same afterward.

She had the newspapers tucked under her arm when she arrived at the office the next morning, but she was in no hurry to look at them, since she had already seen almost more than she cared to on the television news the night before. Nikki North signing the contract, Nikki North bubbling with enthusiasm about moving to Dallas, Nikki North saying that she had "a whole world of confidence" in the guidance of Ben Cameron, her dear, dear friend and adviser.

Jennifer had the papers spread out before her on her desk just inside the entrance. She looked up excitedly when Lee entered.

"Oh, Miss Colder, isn't this the most thrilling thing?" she bubbled. "Aren't these pictures simply wonderful? I think Nikki North is just lovely. And imagine, she's going to be with *our* company! Do you think she'll come here to the office sometime? Oh—you look very nice too, Miss Colder. In the pictures, I mean."

"Thank you, Jennifer," Lee said. She had appeared in one or two of the long shots that took in the whole table where the signing took place, although she had done her best to stay out of camera range.

"You've had some calls already this morning," Jennifer went on. "Delta Distributors in New York—they called twice. And a Mr. Thayer. He's anxious to reach you."

Lee gave a low groan. Dan Thayer managed a number of country singers and singing groups who recorded for WW Music. Impossible to get away from him easily. Still, there was something comforting about getting back to the regular routine of work. And the office did look spotless and orderly after its week of chaos. Maintenance people must have worked overtime, clearing up after the painters, putting everything to rights. Crossing her own office to her desk, Lee felt the plush softness of the new beige carpet under her sandaled feet and reflected that it was surely a pleasanter place now. As fondly attached as she had been to the shabby old offices of WW Music, this was undeniably better. And perhaps with the return of a degree of serenity to their surroundings, she would be able to put her troubled thoughts in order too. She was determined not to let one evening of rash, ill-considered emotion color her whole future, affect her work, destroy her pleasure in a business that had always meant so much to her.

She slipped behind her desk and looked up at the opposite wall, now fresh and immaculate in its new coat of paint. Hanging once again in its accustomed place was Dub's picture, still looking down at her with that secret glint of amusement, that joy of living that she always associated with him. Lee sank back in the plush leather chair with the padded arms and returned the look, wondering as she had so often lately whether she had done the right thing in selling the company, what Dub would have thought of all the changes that were taking place.

She sighed and turned to the messages Jennifer had left for her. Delta Distributors—might as well start with them. She could guess what it was—inquiries about the new North-Garrett releases. How soon will we be able to see some product?

She spent the next forty-five minutes on the telephone, reassuring Delta that they would be the first to know, that they would soon be receiving advance publicity. Two other distributors called from the East Coast. She guessed that she would be receiving calls from California later in the morning when their work day started out there. Reluctantly she dialed Dan Thayer's number. This would take longer, she knew. Dan would be worried about his own clients—artists of lesser magnitude than the new arrivals. His first words confirmed this.

"Listen, Lee honey, I know you're busy there with these two

big Nashville flashes you've signed, but I hope you're not forgetting about the rest of us."

"No, of course not, Dan."

"I've been meaning to get in there to your office, meet the new boss—he's the one with the sayso now, I guess."

"That's right," Lee said stoically. "What's on your mind, Dan?"

"Well, I've been handling a group you recorded a couple of months back—Down Home, they call themselves. You remember them?"

"Certainly I remember them."

"Well, the reason I asked, I thought maybe you'd forgotten about them altogether. You know, they haven't been given any publicity in *Billboard* and the distribution—well, holy smokes, Lee, I'm just back from Atlanta, and not one of the stores there has a single record. I mean, what are you trying to do to my boys?"

"It's been a really hectic time for us, Dan, with the changeover in the company. But things are straightening out now. Just give us another couple of weeks."

"Ought to move while these guys are hot, you know."

"They're really not that hot, Dan," Lee could not resist saying. "But I'll get back to you soon, I promise."

"Well, I sure hope so. Oh, and Lee, while I've got you on the phone, I'm handling a great new singer, name of Loreen Buddly. . . ."

Lee stole a look at her watch. But even with the most tactful stalling and evasion she could not shake Thayer loose before another five minutes had passed. When she did at last replace the phone, she gave a long sigh and ran her fingers through her hair. For the first time she unfolded the newspaper and spread it out on the desk before her, to be confronted by a two-column picture of Nikki North smiling with soft sexiness at Ben Cameron. "Superstars Sign with Dallas Recording Company. Conglomerate Acquisition Opens Door to New Burst of Creative Enterprise in Dallas Area. Cambro Park Opening Set." Her eyes were skimming the headlines when she realized someone had entered the office. She glanced up to see Ben Cameron standing just inside the doorway, seeming, as he always did, to fill the whole room with his height. His face looked pale, his mouth was tight-lipped with anger. His blue eyes seemed to snap with fury and send off sparks that Lee could almost feel.

"Good morning," he said icily. "I see you've read the paper."

"No, actually I haven't, not yet. I've been on the telephone with some distributors and—was there something special—"

"This should interest you." The words dropped jaggedly in the room, sharp-edged and tearing. He crossed to her desk and picked up the newspaper, turning it to the entertainment page.

"Your friend Mr. Tad Summers seems to have done a story on us."

"On us?" she echoed, not understanding. "And who's Tad Summers?"

"He writes a regular column for the paper. He's the one you were exchanging confidences with at the studio."

Lee remembered the young man in jeans and glasses. "Oh. I thought that was another engineer striking up a conversation. Someone who belonged there. I had no idea who it was. Yes, come to think of it, I do know Tad Summers' name, but Steve always deals with the press. I didn't realize—well, what does he say? Certainly it couldn't be anything so dreadful. We were just chatting."

"Well, your little *chat*"—he emphasized the word with elaborate sarcasm—"has netted him quite a bit of information, as you can see."

She scanned the story hurriedly. It was in a column headed "Tapes and Turntables" by Tad Summers, and was prominently placed on the page along with notices of new movies and television shows.

"Is dissension brewing in the offices of the venerable WW Music Company?" the story began. "Personal observation by your reporter indicates that millionaire entrepreneur Ben

Cameron of Cambro, the company's new owner, may have a rebel in the ranks in the person of Miss Lee Colder, former owner of WWM and daughter of the late great W. W. (Dub) Colder, who founded the company."

Lee could feel her hands and feet turning to ice as she skimmed down through the column. Phrases leaped out at her. "In an exclusive interview, Miss Colder confided yesterday . . . all the electronic wonders of the new Cambro studios leave her cold . . . cannot make a hit record, Miss Colder insisted, where talent is lacking . . . Can she be thinking of Nikki North and Joe Bud Garrett, former Nashville superstars now signed with WW Music? This reporter suggests that Mr. Cameron, young takeover wiz with Cambro, may have his hands full with the spirited Miss Colder. . . ."

"But this is dreadful!" Lee exclaimed, dropping the paper. "Ben, I'm so sorry. I had no idea—I didn't know who he was, really. He never introduced himself." Suddenly she remembered the curious look Steve had given him. How could she have been so stupid as to talk so openly to a stranger? "I—I certainly didn't do it on purpose," she stammered. "He was talking about the studio and it was—just casual conversation."

"Nikki will be delighted to hear it."

Lee's heart sank. "Has she seen this?"

"First thing this morning. Her call woke me."

"And she was upset, I suppose."

"I'd say that was a masterpiece of understatement."

"I'll certainly call her and apologize."

His eyes went to the ceiling in a look of desperation.

"Good Lord, the best thing you can do is stay a country mile away from her until she cools down. As it is, this casts a pretty good damper over the reception this week."

He turned away from her and walked to the window, his hands thrust into his pockets. Anger was in every line of the broad shoulders, the set of the jawline which Lee could see obliquely. In spite of herself, Lee could feel an answering anger rising inside her like slow, yeasty bubbles at the unfairness of his accusations.

She said, trying to remain reasonable, "I don't believe that for a minute. It's the kind of thing people read and forget. The best thing is not to pay any attention to it, not to give it any importance."

He whirled around to face her. "But you meant it, didn't you? Those things you told Summers?"

His tone rasped against her with its cutting edge. The bubbles inside her began to boil angrily.

"Yes I did," she replied, returning his look with cold deliberateness. "I meant every word. My father always demanded the highest standard of performance from himself. He didn't always get it from others, I admit, but it was still what he lived by. And I consider that more important than any twenty-four-track board or Jacuzzi tub," she added bitterly.

"Well, those high standards didn't keep the company from nearly going under, did they?" he asked sharply. His eyes bored into her with steely directness.

"Does that mean they ought to be thrown out now?"

He spread both hands palms up in a gesture of exasperation. "Lee, I'm not throwing anything out—least of all quality. I simply want to bring this company into the 1980s. And you're fighting me every step of the way. I don't see how fine engineering and improved studio techniques can do anything but help us."

Lee got up slowly from her desk and stood there quietly, her anger collapsing, suddenly overwhelmed with regret and holding herself firmly in hand to prevent the tears from springing up. The regret was genuine, and it invaded every part of her—regret for something she could not even name, but that she knew had ended before it ever had a chance to begin. She could feel, as tangible as a taut line stretched between them, the powerful attraction he exerted on her, the sensual maleness that she responded to even as she fought against it. And it made no difference that she had told herself over and over these past few days that their relationship could never go beyond business and the casual association of the office. Underneath, where the heart pounded and the blood coursed wildly, the longing and need for him still lingered, no matter how she might deny it to herself. But now—now she had destroyed it completely—unwittingly, but still effectively. He felt that she had set herself up against him publicly, and there was nothing she could say that would change that.

She gave her head a slight shake and said, "I'm sorry, Ben. I do apologize. I'm very sorry it happened."

"Unfortunately that doesn't help much, does it?" he snapped, and his eyes dismissed her with the indifferent glance of a stranger.

CHAPTER SIX

At four o'clock on Thursday afternoon Buffie looked up from her desk as Lee passed and said thoughtfully, "You know, I really should have a dress to wear to that reception."

Lee stopped short and stared at the older woman.

"Buffie Simmons! Do you mean to tell me you haven't even thought about it yet? The reception's day after tomorrow!"

"Well, that's it," Buffie admitted uneasily. "And tomorrow is going to be a pretty busy day. So perhaps I should go look for something now. But my goodness, how long does it take to buy a dress?"

Lee shook her head in despair. "But sometimes dresses have to be altered, Buffie. You shouldn't have left it till the last minute."

"Well, I was thinking of wearing that green thing I wore to my niece's wedding, but then I remembered something got spilled down the front of it—"

Lee took the pencil out of Buffie's hand firmly. "Get going," she said. "In fact, maybe I'd better come with you to supervise." There was a real danger, she thought, that Buffie, who cared not at all for clothes, would buy the first thing off the rack even if it was totally unsuitable.

"Oh, Lee, I'd love that. Only I was going to ask a favor of you. I've almost finished getting together this list of oldies for Mr. Cameron. He wants it for a radio and television package offer. And I promised I'd have it on his desk when he got back. But we need at least twelve songs, and I'm two or three short. I was going back to the storeroom to look over the tapes there. Some things that might not be on my list. If you wouldn't mind doing that—I don't know where Steve is, but he might give you a hand with it when he comes back. Then I could just duck out and find something."

"Fine. I'll get right on it," Lee promised hastily. She had a moment's vision of Buffie falling back on the "green thing" she had worn to her niece's wedding. "Now do look them over carefully, Buffie. Blue looks very nice with your hair, or aqua might be good."

Buffie got up from her desk, nodding and frowning, thinking it over. "I've always liked pink," she said reflectively.

Lee shook her head in despair but managed to maneuver Buffie out of the office with encouragement and numerous warnings about color and style. "Something plain, Buffie," she admonished, and closed the door on her. When she turned back, leaning for a moment against the door, she met Jennifer's glance and the two of them smiled. Lee glanced at her watch.

"Has everyone else left too?" she frowned. "It seems very quiet around here."

"Let me see." Jennifer consulted her daily appointment book. "Mr. Cameron is with Miss North. I believe they were to discuss material for her first album. Steve and Mr. Garrett have gone out together to buy a car."

"A car! Which one is doing the buying?"

"Mr. Garrett. Steve said he just made up his mind rather suddenly and asked Steve if he'd take him around looking."

"Well! I'm going to be working back in the files for an hour or so. No more appointments?"

Jennifer glanced at the book again. "No, nothing more today, Miss Colder."

"All right. You may as well take off a little early, Jennifer." It occurred to Lee that perhaps she should have sent Jennifer shopping with Buffie, but the result might have been a bit too much glamor and high-powered chic for Buffie. Better to leave it to fate and hope for something reasonably suitable.

"Thanks, Miss Colder. See you in the morning then."

When Lee was alone in the office, she gave a sigh of relief and headed back toward the storeroom, turning off lights as she went, still not able to believe that there was no longer a need to economize. She could not have said why she needed to be alone, why she had gone to such pains to send Jennifer home and Buffie shopping. Perhaps because the last two days had been, for her, so packed with tension and discomfort that she longed for the freedom to walk through the office without pretense, to put away from her if only for a few minutes the mask of business-as-usual which she had been wearing ever since the bitter confrontation with Ben Cameron over the Tad Summers column.

Being so near to him, feeling more than ever the powerful attraction he held for her, she could not help reminding herself over and over that she had handled everything wrong from the very beginning. From the moment she met him she had resisted his ideas for rescuing the company. Worse, she had tactlessly expressed her own opinions to Summers, and even though she had not realized he was a reporter, it was still inexcusable; her private opinions should have remained just that—private. She had created an awkward situation for Ben, had been responsible for uncomfortable publicity just when he most needed a smooth start to his tenure as head of WW Music. She had caused severely ruffled feelings in Nikki North, although she could not help observing to herself with some irony, it did appear that Ben had been able to smooth those over. Indeed, he had been with Nikki almost constantly ever since.

And that too, Lee reminded herself severely, was none of her business.

She reached the door to the storeroom at the end of the hall and opened it, slipping inside and turning on the lights so that the metal shelves and storage bins were illuminated. Here were tapes piled on tapes, folders, records, old pressings, newer releases, all arranged chronologically from the earliest days of the company. Lee took a deep breath, inhaling the welcome odor of the place—the only room in the office that had not been done over, the only corner free of fresh paint. Moving its contents to paint it had looked insurmountable, and

Lee was glad it had been left alone. Here at least some remnant of the past remained, some memory of the way things had been once, before it all started to turn sour. For a few minutes she walked among the shelves, running her finger along them, seeing famous names and titles, remembering which ones had launched the company. Dub Colder had his own shelf—rows of titles, stacks of tapes.

Lee returned to the present problem and consulted the list Buffie had handed her. Three more songs. Lee tried to think which ones would make a good addition to those Buffie had already picked. One of Dub's, perhaps. It would help sell an album if his name were included. She would get to that in a minute. But meantime, perhaps one of Tom Traynor's—he was an old friend of Dub's, and even though his records hadn't done as well as Dub had hoped, there were one or two of undeniable quality. Concentrating on the task before her, Lee began pulling out tapes at random, making notes. She turned on the tape player and played some of them over, listening critically, reviewing. Then she moved to Dub's shelf. No need to listen to these, she knew them all by heart. It was only a matter of deciding which to use.

One of the boxes protruded on its shelf, stuck out beyond the others. Lee tried to push it in, found it wedged. Irritated, she pulled it all the way out and put her hand in to see what was there. Something was stuck at the back of the shelf. She pulled it out. A tape in a box that bore the label, W.W.C., and a date six years back.

Lee frowned and turned it over in her hand. On the back of the case a label had been stuck with eight titles listed. Not one of them was familiar to her. For a heart-stopping moment the past came back to Lee. Her father coming in the door, calling out, "Hey, honey, come listen to this new one!" Was it possible? Had Dub really put eight new songs on tape the year before he died and never told her about it? The implications of what such a discovery could mean flooded over Lee. The company might have gone downhill, but Dub's music had not. To the day he died his records had been at the top of the charts. After he died, they had remained there—there had never been a falling off in the demand for music by Dub Colder. If he had, in secret, recorded eight original songs, the news of their discovery would be a sensation in the music world.

Realization overwhelmed Lee, understanding of what it was she held in her hand. It was Dub's legacy—all he had had to leave her that was of value. Something to offset all the mistakes, all the bad management, all the personal failings. Something for her. For a moment she was too overcome with emotion to do anything but stand there clutching the box in both hands. Then with fingers that trembled slightly she opened it, removed the tape, and adjusted it onto the player. She adjusted the volume and stood there waiting.

Soft chords sounded from a familiar guitar, and then a remembered voice with simple country accents said, "This first song's called 'Truckin' South.' " Lee stood transfixed, unable to move, listening to Dub sing of the lonely highways and the big rigs, a subject he had always loved. "Checkin' on the road map, watchin' for the speed trap, burnin' rubber all the way. . . ." She shook her head, smiling faintly and catching her lower lip in her teeth, still not quite believing. Then when the last chords had died away, there was a pause on the tape and then a change of mood, an up-tempo, swingy song full of the youthful joy that had always seemed to make Dub Colder ageless. "Every girl should have a love song—written especially for her. . . ."

Lee, standing rigid, her two hands pressed together, began to relax as she always had under the spell of Dub's voice. Slowly she sank down into a straight chair and leaned forward slightly as she listened. The tape unwound, spinning itself out in soft songs and lively ones, songs that called for country dancing, songs of joy and of sadness. And finally, near the end, a pause and then Dub's speaking voice again saying, "This last one is for someone special. It's called 'Ticket to Home.' "

Lonely chords sounded from the guitar, plaintive notes that spoke of the blues and homesickness. And then the haunting voice again, "Packed my guitar and here's my fare; just give me a ticket to anywhere . . . I can't find a town that doesn't get me down; I'm going home . . . going home to Bonnie Lee. . . ."

"That's you, isn't it?" a voice behind her said.

Lee whirled around, not realizing that tears were streaming down her cheeks.

"Bonnie Lee Colder is you, isn't it?" Ben said. He stood there, arms folded, leaning against the closed door of the storeroom. She thought he must have been there listening for several minutes. His expression was not the closed, tight look of the past few days. It was soft and searching as though there were something he wanted to understand.

"Yes." Her voice was low, scarcely audible over the tape. She moved to turn it off, but he put up a hand to stop her. "Leave it," he said. Neither of them spoke again until the song was over. Then Lee got up, rewound the tape and turned the player off. She removed the tape and for a moment stood there staring at it, turning it over in her hands.

"I just found it," she whispered. "I never knew it existed. They're all songs I never heard before."

"When did he make it?"

"The year before he died, apparently." Lee turned to face him. And now all the coldness, all the animosity had melted away between them, crowded out by the wonder of this discovery. "If you knew," she said in a faltering voice. "If you only knew what this means to me."

"I think I can guess," he said quietly. "Why do you think he never told you about it?"

She paused, seeking in her own mind the answer to this. "I think he was afraid that if he did, I would urge him to put it in an album, and perhaps he worried that the money from it would have to be put back into the company to take care of obligations—I don't know, really, except that I think he just wanted to keep it intact, so that someday—perhaps when I needed it badly—it would be there, like money in the bank. It was a sort of insurance policy for me, I suppose. It was all he had to leave, you see."

He nodded, thinking about it. "Then it should be the first release of the *new* WW Music Company," he said decisively. "An album by Dub Colder—what could be more appropriate?"

She gave him a look that had turned suddenly radiant.

"Ben, do you mean it? Oh, but that would be wonderful!" She was all at once aware of the two of them standing there together in the deserted office, in this miraculous moment no longer enemies. It gave her a tremulous, uncertain feeling.

"I didn't know you were coming back here," she said. "I was just trying to help Buffie out with the list she was making. . . ."

He seemed busy with his own thoughts, not noticing her confusion. "Of course I know you don't think much of the new studio," he said, giving her a wry look that was part amusement. "Even so, I do think Ed Farraday could put the tape through the equalizer and bring up Dub's tones, improve the fidelity of it, make it sound more polished."

"Yes, of course, I understand that. And Ben, I never really meant—I mean, about that column Tad Summer wrote—it was never my intention to cause you any embarrassment."

"Oh, forget it, Lee." His smile, easy and intimate, made her heart stop for a beat. "I'm afraid I overreacted. And Nikki was upset, but I think she's over it now. Let's put it behind us. This is a really exciting discovery."

"I'm so pleased you think so," she said happily. "And if Ed Farraday could bring up the sound and give it more clarity, I'm all for it."

He thrust his hands deep in his pockets and walked over to her. He seemed to be turning something over in his head. She had come to recognize that curious concentration of his. Hesitantly, she put a hand out to touch his sleeve.

"Of course we might be able to do still more with it," he said slowly. "A touch of today's sound might add a lot. That is, leave Dub's voice as it is, of course, and his guitar, but it wouldn't be hard to put another voice over it—someone singing with him.

And after all, we've just signed two major recording stars. This might be a great way to introduce Nikki on our label."

"Nikki North?" Lee echoed. She could hear the hollow sound of her own voice, and her hand came away from his arm.

"Why not? With Dub Colder's voice right there, just as it is but with Nikki singing over it. I'd discuss it with our marketing people, of course, but personally, I like the idea." He glanced at the thin gold watch on his wrist. "I'm supposed to pick Nikki up for dinner soon—I can talk it over with her tonight. We can start moving on this right away."

Lee struggled to stay reasonable, not wanting to give way to the anger that was rising inside her.

"I can understand the need to improve the sound, of course," she said. "The new engineering techniques would do a good job on it, I'm sure. Although Dub managed to sell a great many records without ever being put through an equalizer or anything else." Anger was creeping in. She tried to control it. "But surely it wouldn't be right to change the style —the whole spirit of his music. Dub's appeal was based on that, his popularity came from it. To try to change it simply because we have the capability to do it—that would be a dreadful mistake. In fact, I'm afraid I just couldn't give permission for anything like that." A flush had risen to her face; green eyes snapped at him.

His own face changed ominously. Tight lines appeared at the corners of his mouth and his eyes narrowed. He returned her look coldly. "Permission?" he said. "I don't need your permission."

She held tight to the tape. He glanced at it and added, "And I suggest you don't try to remove that from the office."

"But it's mine!" she stormed.

In an icy voice with all traces of intimacy gone, he said, "Perhaps you'd better consult an attorney about that, Lee."

CHAPTER SEVEN

Lee took a step backward and tilted her head slightly to one side.

"Will it do, do you think?" Buffie asked worriedly. She stood in the middle of Lee's living room, shoulders sagging a bit dejectedly. "It isn't aqua or blue of course, but . . ."

It was, in fact, a rather aggressive shade of rose, but it could have been worse, Lee decided silently. Yet something about it needed pulling together; it had an altogether limp, just-off-the-rack look.

"Yes, of course it will do," she answered brightly. "I think it's exactly right, Buffie. Only perhaps it just needs a couple of touches—"

"That's what I thought," Buffie agreed, looking relieved. "That's why I wanted to come over here and dress so that you could give me a hand with it. You're so good at things like that, Lee."

Lee was thinking rapidly. It was a fairly simple dress, luckily. Buffie had, this time, avoided the ruffles, scarves, and over-skirts which she was apt to succumb to. And its mandarin collar offered a chance for a necklace. Long full sleeves, also good, Lee decided. But it needed something to keep it from looking so shapeless. She glanced at the slim gold watch on her wrist. Typical of Buffie to leave all this until the last minute. Steve would be here to pick them up soon. She herself had been ready for a half hour. She was feeling suddenly shy and uncomfortable about the whole business of the reception, and there was bitterness mixed in as well, she had to admit. She and Ben Cameron had avoided each other all the next day after their encounter in the storeroom. It had not been hard to do, since he had been in the office only briefly. Most of his time had been taken up in attentions to Nikki North. But today, Lee knew, there could be no dodging of her responsibilities. She had to appear at the reception, see that everything ran smoothly, had to be cordial to Nikki, had to confront Ben Cameron before the whole world—which meant being cordial to him too. Well, if it was something that had to be done—and it was—she could do it, Lee told herself. Even so, she was grateful that Steve had offered to drive them. It would be easier, she thought, with Steve and Buffie along.

She was becoming quite adept at hiding her true feelings these days, Lee admitted to herself with some irony. After a lifetime of speaking her mind honestly as Dub had always encouraged her to do, she now found herself in a world of big business—a world of deals, of estimates, of calculated risks, of profit margins. In that world success rather than honesty was what counted. What was said one day could be turned around 180 degrees the next so that it came out as something else entirely. Ben Cameron had obviously mastered these techniques already, she thought. Or perhaps he had been born with the skills needed to master them. Lee was finding it hard to do. And hardest of all was having to accept the dull pain that came with knowing that even her father's music, which she had always thought was as unchanging as the Texas landscape itself, now belonged to someone else—someone who was planning to change it drastically, and had the right to do so.

She tried hard to steer her thoughts away from other aspects of the situation, from the warm, sensual memory of Ben's arms around her, the low caressing tone of his voice. "I had to come back. I had to . . . I had to see you again—to hold you. . . ." Even as her eyes misted over, Lee swallowed hard and gave herself a tiny shake, trying to put the recollection away from her, trying to bring herself back to the present and to reality. For that was never reality, she reminded herself. Reality is what I must face now—today. . . .

"What do you think?" Buffie was asking.

"What?" Lee forced her attention back to now. "Oh—the

dress. Well, silver might do. I think it would go well with that color. Let me see what I can find." She hurried into the bedroom and began rummaging through her things. At last she located a necklace in dull silver, not too heavy for the dress, and a soft silver-fabric belt, wide and pliable. Buffie's waistline took up most of it, but Lee managed to get it around her and fastened. "Don't eat too much, Buffie," she warned with a smile.

"I'll be careful," Buffie said seriously, and then added, "What do you think about my hair?"

Lee surveyed it, gave a sigh, and went looking for a brush.

Ten minutes later when Steve appeared at the door, he gave a low, admiring whistle at the sight of Lee in her dress of jade-green silk—one of the purchases she had made at the small, exclusive shop in the Galleria. The design was simple and elegant—thin spaghetti straps at the shoulders, a slender belted waist, tiny pleats forming the skirt. Her hair fell softly to her shoulders.

"Hey, what are you trying to do, knock 'em dead?" he asked, planting a kiss on her cheek. "Buffie, my love, you are a vision of delight," he exclaimed, catching sight of her over Lee's shoulder. Practical Buffie blushed furiously, and Lee teased Steve, "Lucky you, showing up with two beauties in tow."

"Don't think I don't appreciate it."

"Well, you look very grand yourself," Lee said, taking a step backward for a better view. Steve obligingly made a full turn to show off his dark slacks, leather Western-style jacket, bolo tie with its silver ornament, and silver belt buckle.

"And honestly, Steve, I am grateful. I'm surprised you didn't want to take a real date to this thing."

"This *thing?*" he said, raising his eyebrows. "Not a very respectful way to refer to our big social debut. And as far as a date is concerned, today I'm playing the field. Can't limit myself to one girl at this kind of affair. I want to give 'em all a chance. So look, you two won't mind if after things get under way—well, you know—"

"Oh, I get it. Once you've delivered us, you're dumping us, right?" Lee said, mock-serious.

"I wouldn't have said 'dump.' "

"Never mind, we get the picture. And you don't have to worry about seeing us home, either, if something better turns up. We can manage for ourselves. Just getting us there is enough."

Exchanging lighthearted banter with Steve, giving last touches to Buffie's hair and dress, casting a quick look in the mirror at her own image, Lee tried to keep her spirits up, her mind away from the very real dread with which she had been approaching this day. But when Steve called out, "All right, you two lovelies, let's get going!" the crushing oppressive weight of it came down around her. She would be entering a world completely foreign to her—sophisticated, glittering, shot through with all the attributes of wealth and power. It was never Dub's world and it's not mine, she thought in sudden desperation. I won't fit in—I don't even want to. With grim determination she kept her thoughts away from Ben Cameron. *That* part of it didn't even bear thinking about. She had no idea what would happen when the two of them faced each other again. Except that Ben Cameron would never do anything to upset a day this important. He would carry it off with grace and nonchalance, as if they were on the best of terms.

"Life used to be so simple," she murmured as Steve held the door open for them. "When people knew where they stood and everybody said what he really meant."

His eyes widened with surprise, and she realized she had expressed her inner thoughts aloud without meaning to. "Oh —you know what I mean," she added, flustered.

"Well, no, not exactly," Steve admitted. "But look, Lee." He took her by the arm and detained her a moment as Buffie moved out ahead of them. "Give the guy a chance, why don't you? I mean, he's only doing what he feels will help the company."

"I know," Lee said with a kind of dull acceptance. Then she

brightened deliberately. "Hey, don't listen to me. I must be in a mood today."

"Go on," he joked. "Nobody who looks as good as you do has a right to be in any kind of mood—except up."

"Then that's what I'll be—up," she promised.

"Attagirl. Come on now, let's get moving. We're supposed to be there early, you know. Hey, wait till you see the new car Garrett bought. . . ."

Cambro Business Park, even though still unfinished in some sections, had in honor of today's occasion been given so much loving attention by landscape gardeners and grounds keepers, by decorators and maintenance people, that now, in the last of the late-afternoon sun's long rays, it had an almost magical appearance, with the ten-story San Carlos Hotel towering over the other low, modular structures like the turreted castles Lee remembered from the fairy tales she had once read.

The low, clustered buildings had been artfully built among existing trees. Man-made streams and ponds enhanced the natural look of the site, and all the buildings were reachable by car or along footpaths that wound through the landscape. Small, discreetly lettered signs pointed out directions: TO STUDIO, TO CAMBRO OFFICES, TO GOLF COURSE. Around the lush green of the golf course itself, visible in the distance as they drove up, a number of luxury homes had been built. Lee supposed they would later be occupied by various executives and their families.

All the way there in Steve's car Lee had felt her own mood undergoing a change. What she had been dreading became, under the prodding of habit and an ingrained sense of responsibility, a challenge to be met, a job to be done well. Out of her handbag came lists and notes, and by the time they got out of the car in front of the hotel, she felt totally in command of herself, ready to oversee arrangements, to make sure every detail of the day was perfect. She allowed herself a moment or two of looking around, taking in the delicate beauty of the circular drive that led up to the entrance. It had been done in a stone mosaic patterned to form seashells. Lee, who had been at the hotel the week before to confer with the management about the reception, had noticed its still incomplete look then. But progress had been astonishing in those few days. Now as they entered the hotel lobby, she took note of the sea-foam-green carpeting that covered the whole area. Furniture accents were in peach and beige. Lush plantings seemed to have been placed everywhere—palms, ficus trees, caladiums. The registration desk was tucked out of sight at the left. To the right was the grand ballroom. Several hotel guests mingled in a cozy sitting area with a small bar which was straight ahead across the lobby, and Lee knew, although all were not visible from here, that a number of restaurants also occupied this main floor, all opening onto lawns, streams, ponds, and gardens.

She could hear beside her Buffie's sharp intake of breath as she saw it all for the first time. Lee decided prompt action was called for before Buffie drifted into a hopeless trance at the contemplation of so much luxury and beauty.

"Buffie dear, will you do something for me?" she said briskly. "Before everyone starts arriving, will you take this menu and the seating plans and go over them with the kitchen and the maitre d'? I'm sure everything's absolutely perfect, but we must be sure. Steve, you watch for the first arrivals here. Where do you suppose Ben and the guests of honor are?"

"Suite upstairs," Steve said. "The company has private rooms on the top floor. But they'll be down soon."

Lee could feel a warm flush tingling along her arms. "Good," she said, keeping her voice matter-of-fact. "Before they appear, I'd better look around. The plan is to receive people at the arbor out in the garden. I want to look it over and see whether it's going to be too breezy out there. Women don't appreciate it if their hairdos get blown around."

Buffie, who had been looking anxious, said, "Chefs and maitre d's can be terribly cross, Lee. You don't think they'll mind my snooping around—"

"Buffie Simmons!" Lee gave her a stern look. "WW Music is paying for this bash. Have you forgotten that you're the company's director of operations and business administration?"

"That's so," Buffie agreed hesitantly. "Well then. I'll just get right after it." She squared her shoulders and crossed the plush lobby, sinking into the carpet with every step on her unfamiliar heels. Lee and Steve exchanged a secret grin.

"Let me go look the situation over," Lee said. "I'll rejoin you right away."

"Be sure you do," Steve warned. "The golfing crowd is sure to show up early. I may not be able to handle it all by myself."

Lee grinned at him, sensing the excitement and anticipation that were making him glow. Steve was at his best with a crowd; it would take more than a few early arrivals to bother him.

"Silly, you know you can handle anything," she teased. "I won't be long," she added, and headed for the huge dining room at the hotel's northwest corner that was to be used for Cambro's dinner guests. She did not linger there. Out of the corner of her eye she could see Buffie in earnest consultation with a man in a white dinner jacket. She seemed to be very much in charge. Her voice came clearly to Lee across the expanse of small tables with their beige, brown, and blue tablecloths which coordinated with the room's color scheme.

"Miss Colder mentioned the one long table near the band? But with everyone facing the guests, of course . . ."

Lee hurried out through the big glass doors that led from the dining room into one of the many gardens surrounding the hotel. Directly outside the doors was a patio, and then lawns stretching down to a decorative pool with an arbor to one side. The lawn was a slope of perfect green, as velvety as the carpet in the lobby. Azaleas and Indian hawthorn spread out in massive plantings down the gentle knoll toward the water. In large, curving beds were sweeps of blue periwinkles and other flowering plants. Across the expanse of lawns and walkways new office buildings still under construction could be seen, but here all was perfection, serenity, completion. As Lee stood

there watching the slow fading of daylight, the perfectly posi-
tioned lights came on, some of them on standards and made to
resemble old-fashioned gaslights, others concealed among the
plantings and lending a subtle illumination to the area. No
wind as yet, she noted, turning back inside. She paused only
long enough to give last-minute instructions regarding the
serving of drinks and canapés outdoors, then hurried back to
the lobby.

Steve had been right, she noted, watching the first of the
guests arrive and seeing Steve step forward to greet them with
outstretched hand. Sure enough, they were a group of golfers,
easily identified by their lime-green or salmon-colored slacks
and plaid sports coats. At the same moment she saw the elevator doors opening in the far corner of the lobby and her heart
gave a leap, but it was Joe Bud Garrett by himself who stepped
out. He looked around, and Lee hurried over to him.

"Hey there, little lady," he said in his down-home way.
"Don't you just look like the prettiest thing south of the Pan-
handle tonight!"

Lee could not help smiling at him. "Well, you're very handsome yourself, Joe Bud." He looked only slightly theatrical in
his leather vest, dark slacks, and Western boots, and Lee found
herself surprisingly glad to see him. There was something
comfortable about Joe Bud in spite of his superstar status. He
was, she decided, an easy person to be with. "And I heard a
great deal about that new car of yours from Steve."

"Oh, honey, that car is a beauty," Joe Bud said with enthusiasm. "I'm taking you out for a ride in it first chance I get."

"I'll look forward to it."

"Found it right on the floor, you know. Somebody else had
ordered it special and then the deal fell through. White Seville
with cowhide upholstery. . . ."

"Steve's terribly impressed."

He glanced over the lobby and asked, "Well, did the others
beat me down? Am I late?"

"No, Ben and Nikki aren't down yet—that is—I thought the

three of you were together," Lee said. Realization was washing over her like a cold rain.

"No, I was in my own room on the ninth floor," Joe Bud said. "They've been up in the penthouse suite for the last couple of hours." He paused and gave her a sharp look. "Well, they had a lot to discuss, you know. Business, I mean."

"Yes. Oh, of course," Lee said, making a concentrated effort to keep her voice light. "I'm sure they'll be along soon." But the numbing cold would not leave her. As she stepped aside with Joe Bud and kept up a light conversation, one part of her felt a sharp, stabbing pain that refused to go away. She had seen, that day in the studio, why audiences loved Nikki. In an immediate flash of understanding she had known what it was about her—the irresistible little-girl look, the appealing air of innocence. Lee, expecting someone brassier, showier, had seen instead a delicate, clinging quality, a thing that had probably worked well in the past when she had been Nola Mae Nettles, Miss Metroplex. Now that she was a rising star, it was still endearing her to the public. Her helpless, wistful look undoubtedly concealed a will of iron—indeed, Lee was sure of it—but it was serving very well to take her where she wanted to go, straight to the top. And that small white hand resting on Ben Cameron's arm—Lee wondered whether Nikki had now set her sights on another goal, the acquisition of a handsome millionaire businessman as a husband. It would be a suitable conquest for someone like Nikki, particularly since Ben had involved himself in record production and could be instrumental in furthering her career. And if this was her goal, what better way to achieve it than to offer a foretaste of future intimacy? Two hours alone in the luxury of the hotel's penthouse suite would be enough, Lee was sure, to achieve the desired result.

Taking a deep breath, Lee tried to hold on to her happy expression and give her attention to what Joe Bud was saying, but a cold, heavy feeling of loss had settled oppressively around her heart. It was nothing to her, she reminded herself, whatever Nikki's goals might be. But one thing she was sure of: girls like Nikki got what they went after.

She heard the soft whir of the elevator doors opening once more and turned toward them as Joe Bud said, "Well now. Here they are at last. We were about ready to give up on you two . . ."

Lee swallowed, feeling a sudden dryness in her mouth, a flush in her face as she faced Nikki and Ben, just emerging from the elevator. Her heart caught, then started to throb wildly at the sight of him in his dark blue sports coat, white shirt, and gray slacks. For a fraction of a second their eyes locked and his gaze raked over her red-gold hair tumbling around her shoulders, the green silk dress clinging to her body. But then at once he looked away from her, glancing around the lobby.

"We haven't kept you waiting, have we?" he said coolly.

"No, of course not," Lee said automatically. "We were having a nice chat. Hello, Nikki. You look simply stunning." She was suddenly thankful for Joe Bud's warm, easy presence. Ben's expression was that of a polite stranger, and it took only one glance at Nikki to tell that while she might not be angry at Ben over the Summers column, she was not going to forgive Lee. The brief look Nikki gave her was venomous, ice-encrusted; the dismissal was absolute. After that her eyes had moved with restless boredom around the lobby. Her outfit proclaimed stardom; Lee could not help looking at it. A two-piece pants ensemble of turquoise silk. The pants were ankle-length and slim. Her turquoise sandals had four-inch heels, but she still came only to Ben's shoulder. Her tunic top had large sleeves and a wide neck. It was worn over the pants and was belted at the waist with a sequined magenta sash. An Indian-style headband around her forehead was of the same sequined magenta and held in place a mass of frosted curls.

Slowly and deliberately then, while Lee watched, Nikki tipped her head up to look at Ben, a long, slow look that was so sensual and explicit, so unmistakably intimate that Lee could feel her own breath catch in her throat. She saw Ben return the look, his head bent to Nikki's, their eyes meeting in a private exchange that was clearer than words. For a moment Lee stood there in a kind of paralysis until Joe Bud offered her his arm and said, "Lead on, pretty lady. We're in your hands tonight, I reckon."

Taking Joe Bud's arm, Lee led the way across the lobby toward the glass doors at the rear. Behind her she could hear Ben's footsteps, his long stride carefully shortened as he escorted Nikki, his voice low and intimate as he spoke to her. She was glad for Joe Bud's sturdy arm to lean on. She felt a trembling inner weakness, and a blur of tears misted her eyes.

CHAPTER EIGHT

From the moment they stepped out onto the patio in the soft Texas twilight, with the lights giving off their hazy golden glow, the whole affair began to turn into one huge, moving blur to Lee. Moments ran together, voices blended, images fused and separated and came together again.

"Absolutely stunning—the surroundings are so natural. . . ."

"I never realized the airport was close by. Didn't take us any time at all once we'd landed. . . ."

"How's the golf course? I hear the dogleg on Number Nine is tough, but then of course . . ."

"I like the service. And these canapés are excellent. I wasn't really pleased with the last caterers I used. . . ."

"Doesn't Nikki North look smashing? I wish I could wear that style. Of course now that I'm on that new diet . . ."

Through it all Lee managed to retain her poise, moving through the crowd holding a glass of champagne which she had not touched, greeting new arrivals as they appeared, and managing to sound as warm and welcoming at the fiftieth encounter as at the first. She knew some of them by sight: wealthy businessmen from Dallas and elsewhere, attorneys and doctors, professional athletes—she thought at least some of the guests might be investors in the Cambro venture. Local radio personnel and station owners, newspaper owners and staff—she caught sight of Tad Summers but managed to dodge him. The mayor, city council members with their husbands and wives, and photographers everywhere along with a television Minicam and accompanying crew. Flashbulbs popped and glared, illuminating the night as the picture takers kept finding new subjects. Ben Cameron shaking hands with the mayor, Nikki with one of the Dallas Cowboys, Joe Bud Garrett with Miss Texas, Nikki and Joe Bud together. At one point Lee's attention came to a focus as she saw Ben posing with two other men—one portly and good-natured-looking, one thinner and sharper-faced. Lee frowned and wondered who they were as the cameras circled them. At the same moment Steve edged through the crowd and seized her elbow.

"Lee! Over this way—Ben wants you to meet . . ."

Lee, following along in a bewildered haze, lost the rest of his words. Then suddenly Steve deposited her at the arbor near the pool, and Ben was saying coolly, "Ah, there you are. Lee, I want you to meet my brothers. This fellow who needs to lose twenty pounds is Frederick, and this one is Philip. They flew down to keep an eye on me tonight—I'm sure you can understand why," he added with a sardonic look, and Lee, reddening, knew that he was still remembering her comment on the first day they met—that he was no doubt the brother who didn't count for much.

"Well, well," Frederick Cameron said as he seized her hand, "you told us how smart she was, Ben. You never said she was a beauty too!" And Philip, quieter and more sedate, shook her hand politely and told her it was a pleasure.

"Now hold on a minute, we want you to meet the girls too," Frederick added heartily, and began looking around. The "girls" proved to be their wives, whose names were Grace and Sondra. Lee had no trouble sorting them out—Frederick's wife was built like him, stout and comfortable, while Philip's was a pencil-thin, stylish woman with a gaunt face.

"How wonderful that you all came tonight," Lee said sincerely.

"Wouldn't have missed it," Frederick assured her. "We think a lot of this boy and his project. Glad he's got somebody with your knowledge and experience to help him out, Miss Colder."

"Lee," she said quickly.

"Well, I do feel kind of as if I know you already—through

your father, that is. Grace and I still listen to his records, don't we, my dear?"

"Oh, indeed we do," pleasant-faced Grace assured her.

For a moment it was hard for Lee to remember that these were people of power and wealth, manipulators of companies, tycoons whose smallest whims sent Wall Street into tailspins. They were simply a family, and they were here tonight because of that relationship. To wish a younger brother well, to look over his shoulder with fraternal interest, approve of his enterprise. Lee felt curiously touched by all of it. They cared—it mattered enough for them to come, she thought, and glanced up to catch Ben's expression. For a fraction of a second their eyes met, but then at once his slid away from her, growing cold with indifference. Nikki North, who had been talking with someone off to his left, moved in close beside him, one arm creeping around his waist, her head tilting toward his shoulder.

"Are we going inside soon, Ben?" she murmured. "I'm getting a tiny bit chilly."

His arm came around her at once, protective and enveloping. Lee turned from them quickly and struggled to keep her voice normal as she invited the older Cameron brothers and their wives to lead the way indoors. "Last time I looked, that buffet table was ready and waiting," she said.

Frederick Cameron and his wife assured her they would be only too happy to start the movement toward dinner, and the two of them began to move off toward the door. Lee was careful not to look in Ben's direction again as she began shepherding guests toward the dining room.

The long buffet table, set up against one wall, quickly became the focus of attention as plates were filled with roast beef, seafood Newburg casserole, rice-and-peas, spinach salad with cheese and hot bacon dressing, and fresh fruit salad in minted yogurt. Lee had purposely kept the menu simple, but all the food had been meticulously prepared and attractively presented. Guests began seating themselves at the small tables. The country band which Lee had engaged was already playing on a platform at one end of the room. In front of it was a long table at which were seated the Cameron brothers and their wives, Ben, Nikki, Joe Bud, Buffie, and Steve. Lee was the last to join the company group after assuring herself that everyone was seated and having a good time. Talk and laughter sounded throughout the room. Waiters circulated, filling and refilling champagne glasses. Lee was seated next to Joe Bud Garrett, who with perfect ease kept up a lively conversation throughout dinner. He remembered Dub Colder well, he told her, although he had been "only a kid" at the time of Dub's great popularity. He had even done his own recorded version of "One More Heartache."

"Oh, but I've heard it!" Lee exclaimed. "You did a very good job on it."

"Just middling," he grinned. "That song belonged to Dub Colder—nobody else could touch it, really. But I got a kick out of doing it."

"Well, Dub would certainly have approved, I know that," she assured him. "He always encouraged younger singers coming along."

As she talked with him, her eyes moved to the other end of the table, where Ben sat between Nikki and Philip Cameron's thin wife. Nikki ate sparingly and spent much of her time posing, tipping her head back to laugh a rippling laugh, waving at various guests who caught her eye. Ben was solicitous and attentive, but managed with extraordinary good grace not to neglect the older woman on the other side.

When the waiters began to move among the diners with trays of pastries and tortes, with coffee, with refills for champagne glasses, one of the band members came to the front of the platform and held up his hands for quiet. Lee thought that Steve must have arranged this part. She smiled at the musician, Eddie Howe, as he caught her eye. She knew all the members of the Mother Lode well; they were a good, solid country group whom she had used often as backup on recording sessions.

"If I may have your attention, folks," Eddie said with a

smile. "I know you'd like a few words from your host, one of country music's newest and most enthusiastic fans, Mr. Ben Cameron!"

Ben smiled at the applause which greeted him, then stood up and stepped in one easy stride onto the platform and walked over to the microphone. Lee looked quickly down at the table, and only after he had started speaking did she stealthily return her eyes to his face. Her cheeks were burning with a color she hoped others were not noticing.

"We're delighted you came," Ben said simply. "WW Music welcomes you all. And before the evening's over we want to be sure you've all looked in on our new studios just across the way." He waved in the direction of the new buildings. "We're very proud of our new facilities and we'd like to show them off. We have great hopes for Dallas as a recording center, and Cambro sees no end to the possibilities for expansion in the entertainment field. At the very heart of that endeavor we are proud to place WW Music, a company founded by an enormous creative talent, Dub Colder, and now to be enhanced by two of America's top country stars, Nikki North and Joe Bud Garrett." He lifted both hands, palms up, in a gesture indicating the two stars, and there was another wave of applause. Nikki smiled dazzlingly and blew a kiss in Ben's general direction; Joe Bud smiled in quick professional acknowledgment.

"And incidentally, if anyone here hasn't yet met them, we want to be sure you do that too before leaving," Ben went on smoothly. As the applause died away, he went on with enthusiasm, "What we really feel optimistic about is starting with Dub Colder's great legacy—being able to combine it with today's creative recording techniques and the great new technology embodied in our studios. We hope that some of the best music will soon be coming out of Dallas, because we certainly plan to give Nashville some healthy competition." Once again he was interrupted by applause. Only after the big room was quiet again did he go on, and now his voice took on a slightly different tone—emphatic yet quietly serious. "And now I have an announcement of particular importance to make." The hush

deepened in the dining room, broken only by the quiet movement of waiters and an occasional clink of a cup against a
saucer. "Recently in our office we discovered a heretofore
unreleased tape of Dub Colder singing eight original songs."
He paused to let the news sink in, and from several parts of the
room came small, surprised gasps. "I want to announce to you
all tonight that this will be our first release. Dub's own voice
will be heard again, and his inimitable style will be enhanced
by some additional backup music and by the voice of the
lovely Miss North, which will be added to his on the record."

Applause and cheers swept the dining room again, but suddenly all Lee could hear was a voice in her memory. Words
and phrases from that scene in the storeroom came back to
her. *That's you, isn't it?* . . . *Bonnie Lee Colder is you* . . .
first release of the new WW Music . . . *a touch of today's
sound* . . . *a great way to introduce Nikki* . . ." And then
coldly: *Perhaps you'd better consult an attorney about
that.* . . .

She realized Ben had held up his hands for quiet. "And don't
think we've forgotten Mr. Joe Bud Garrett, either. He and
Miss North will do an album together, and we're putting together an album for him alone with all new material."

While the applause went on, rising in waves around her, Lee
kept her eyes down, refusing to look up at him, although some
instinct told her that his blue eyes were seeking her out. But
seeking her out for what purpose, she thought bitterly. Only to
gloat, to remind her that the decisions were his to make, not
hers. To flaunt his power. Resolutely she refused to react to
him in any way that would give him satisfaction. Glancing
around the table, she was surprised to find Frederick Cameron
looking at her with thoughtful, penetrating eyes, his plump,
good-humored features drawn into a speculative expression.
Uneasily she turned to Joe Bud Garrett to murmur congratulations.

"Sounds wonderful," she told him. "I know you're going to
make a hit."

But once again Ben was motioning for quiet. "One last introduction, folks!" he said with a smile. "It wouldn't be complete tonight if I didn't introduce the heart—and most of the brains —of WW Music. Dub's own daughter, Miss Lee Colder!"

For a moment Lee felt paralyzed with shock and could only sit rigidly in her chair. Then Joe Bud Garrett leaned toward her and said encouragingly, "Take a bow, honey—that applause is for you."

Slowly she stood up, squaring her shoulders. Of course that flowery introduction was all for the benefit of the crowd. Good public relations for the company. Even so, she was Dub Colder's daughter, and proud of it. She smiled at the crowd, lifted one hand in a small wave, and then for the first time since he had started speaking, turned to Ben. He leaned forward, offering her his hand to help her up the step to the platform. There was no way to avoid it. She took his hand and with one light step joined him at the microphone. He adjusted it downward for her and again motioned the crowd to silence.

"Thank you all," she said in a firm, quiet voice. "And special thanks to Cambro, and to all the Camerons whom I've met tonight, for the chance to carry on my father's company. I can't tell you . . ." She hesitated, but she knew what had to be said, what she was obligated to say. "I can't tell you how happy I am that Dub Colder's last work is to be recorded." Once again, curiously, her eyes fell on Frederick Cameron and that probing, penetrating look. For a moment she faltered, not knowing what else to say, but Ben chimed in quickly, "And now, how would you like to hear this fine country band play some of Dub's music?"

This time the applause rocked the room and voices shouted, "One More Heartache!" Ben turned to Eddie Howe, and Eddie nodded. Lee, still at the microphone, said suddenly, "We have someone here who made a very fine recording of that song himself. Wouldn't you like to hear Joe Bud Garrett sing it?" Cheers and clapping answered, and Joe Bud jumped up to join the band, slipping one arm around Lee's waist and waving to the guests.

"My record could never measure up to Dub's," he said good-naturedly, "but I'd be real happy to oblige."

It was at that moment, amidst all the laughter and cheering, that Lee happened to glance at Nikki, at the other end of the table, and realized that she had made a serious blunder. Nikki was sitting there with a fixed smile on her face, but angry color had risen to her cheeks and her resentment could be read plainly.

Hastily Lee rallied and said over the general hubbub, "And how about lovely Nikki North? A little harmony from her would certainly enhance—"

But a sudden change of expression from Nikki stopped her. It moved in an instant from petulant annoyance to pure panic. She flushed an even deeper hue and held up both hands, diamonds flashing, and said in her most winning tones, "No, no, I'm on vacation right now. I'll be put to work soon enough."

"Oh, come on, Nikki!" a voice from a far corner shouted, and others took it up. Lee, seeing the consternation on Nikki's face, understood it now. While Nikki had resented losing the spotlight, even briefly, she had no desire to sing. For the moment it did not matter why. It mattered only that she herself had made a tactless mistake. And how was she to undo it? While the shouting, applause, laughter continued, Ben whirled on her, his back to the microphone, and said furiously, "What the devil are you trying to do, embarrass Nikki? She doesn't want to get up here and sing without any rehearsal."

"I'm so sorry," Lee murmured wretchedly. "I never thought—I mean, everybody knows the song—"

"Well, since you got us into this, I suggest you get us out of it," he hissed angrily in her ear. "Why don't *you* do the singing with Joe Bud if you think harmony will *enhance* things?"

The crowd had grown quieter, sensing something wrong, even though they could not hear what was being said.

"I'm no singer," Lee retorted in a low voice.

His mouth curled sardonically. "Well, if not, it's the only thing you've admitted you can't do."

Lee felt her own lips tightening with anger. She turned to Joe Bud, who was regarding her with the wise, experienced eyes of a seasoned performer. Casually he said, "Come on, honey. You and me. How about it?"

Once again Ben held up his hands for silence. "It's all right," he assured them all. "We're going to let Nikki enjoy her vacation. Miss Lee Colder will sing her father's music with Joe Bud."

The crowd, well-fed, happy, ready to enjoy whatever came along, cheered again and sank slowly into quiet, with scattered talk, laughter, and movement. Ben jumped down, giving a signal to lower a few of the lights. A spotlight came on, focusing on the two figures standing in front of the band as the musicians started to play.

What she had said was true; she had never thought of herself as a singer, had never entertained any aspirations toward becoming one. Luckily Dub's music was simple, straightforward, honest, and she sang it that way—as she always had when she was at home with no one to hear. Being in the spotlight, in the hushed, crowded room, could do nothing to turn her into an instant professional and she knew it, but Joe Bud Garrett's sure, confident baritone carried them both along. As they sang together Lee began to feel more sure of herself and was even able to slip into a high, sweet harmony on the chorus. "One more heartache doesn't matter, I still love you—and every time you leave I feel the same—"

Make the words matter, Dub had always said; she had told Ben it was why his music lasted. At the very core of it was a strain of wistful sadness, but no song of his was without the hope, the bouncing-back quality that was the essence of all good country music. Hanging on, no matter what. "I may be a fool, but I'll take you back again," they sang, and Eddie Howe's fiddle took up the melody as the voices left off, to be answered by the guitar and the soft, sliding notes of the steel.

The applause crashed over them like thunder before the music had died away. Joe Bud leaned over and kissed her soundly on the cheek, raising her hand high to acknowledge the crowd's enthusiasm along with him, hugging her, bowing to the audience and then to her.

"Hey, honey, that was great!" he shouted in her ear over the din. He helped her down off the platform, and she moved with some difficulty through the crowd, all on their feet now. As she passed close to Nikki, the singer turned her back deliberately, and Lee had a moment's anxiety about having made an ugly situation still worse, if that was possible. She did not see Ben in the crowd. Then almost at once she was being jostled, congratulated, hugged, and it was several minutes before she could escape the press of people and duck into a small adjoining room back of the bandstand. It was where the musicians had left their cases and for the moment no one was in it. She heard the band starting to play again and the noise and laughter of the crowd breaking apart, moving, talking, reluctant to end the evening. Slowly, feeling drained emotionally, Lee moved to a window and leaned with her head against the glass, standing there for several minutes, waiting for the excitement and the keyed-up feeling to dissipate, knowing she should be back there saying last cordial words to the guests, but feeling relief in the small room's peaceful quiet.

"Very nice, Miss Colder," said a voice from the doorway suddenly, knifing into the silence and making her heart jump. She whirled around to see Ben standing there with the light and noise behind him. He closed the door and they stood alone in the stillness. "*Very* nice," he repeated. "And well engineered too. I didn't realize you had aspirations to stardom." His blue eyes raked her coldly.

"But I never—I didn't—you were the one who—" Lee found herself sputtering ineffectually, so stunned by the unfairness of his accusations that she could hardly put her words together.

"I should have realized it—everyone wants to be a star. Well, it was a nice stunt you pulled up there. No wonder you wanted to hire the band yourself. Of course you figured Nikki wouldn't want to get up and sing without any preparation—"

"But it was all your idea!" she cried. "And besides, I didn't think that! I didn't think about it at all, actually. If I had," she could not help adding with some irony, "I'm afraid I would have assumed that she was enough of a pro to do just that—get up and sing. I'm afraid I forgot that Miss North is one of the new breed—not able to perform without all conditions being favorable and the wind from the southwest—"

"That's not fair!" he shouted angrily. "Simply because she wants to do her best work always—"

"And show herself off to the best possible advantage—"

"What's wrong with that?"

Lee felt a lump forming in her throat; tears sprang hotly to her eyes. Her shoulders sagged and she felt an enormous weariness all over. But she was determined not to show weakness before him.

"Nothing, I suppose," she said quietly. For a moment neither one spoke. Then into the silence Lee said, "Interesting to see how you Camerons work. Not only do you come in and take over, trampling everyone who gets in your way, but you manage to take a perfectly innocent situation and turn it around so that someone else has to shoulder the blame. Very neat, but it must take some practice. I don't think I could ever master the technique."

"Oh, you're doing very well on your own," he said in a voice thin and sharp with cynicism.

Lee felt all at once weak and trembling, all her defenses down, all arguments defeated before she could voice them. Without her willing it, memory sprang back and she could feel the warm sensual pressure of those lips on hers, the hard muscular strength of that body as he crushed her to him. She was overwhelmed with a powerful sense of loss, but what she had lost was something she had never had, really. It had not meant anything to him, and she had been a fool to let it mean anything to her. Well, that could be remedied, she thought bitterly. She could cut him out of her heart like a bruised spot cut from a peach. And that was all it was, actually. A bruise. Not fatal—she would survive it, she told herself resolutely, trying not to remember how that kiss had felt.

"You've embarrassed Nikki," he muttered angrily. "I'll have my work cut out for me making *that* right."

"Oh, I'm sure it won't be difficult for you," she said sweetly.

"And if you think this will have any effect on plans for the recording session with her, you're wrong."

"I never for a moment thought you'd admit *that* was a bad idea," Lee snapped. "You're not the type to confess to a mistake."

"I don't consider it a mistake!" he shouted furiously.

"Ah yes, I remember. Profit's the name of the game."

"Unless you come up with something better, yes, it is," he replied, his voice suddenly icy cold. The silence was frosted with it now, the gap between them as wide as the Rio Grande. He made a move to leave, then turned back to her. "I'm assuming you still work for this company," he said in a stranger's voice. "If so, I'd like to remind you that the party's over now. We have an album to cut. I expect you to be there next week with us to help Nikki learn the new songs. I'm assuming you're enough of a team player to do that."

Lee met his gaze levelly, not flinching.

"Of course I am," she said coolly. "You don't need to worry. I'll be there."

CHAPTER NINE

Since Steve was by now giving his total attention to a blond girl in a white strapless gown, it was a Dallas Cowboy, finally, who insisted on taking Lee home. The tall athlete's very name would have started many a girl's heart pounding, but Lee found herself struggling to make even polite conversation with him as they drove. She had left the San Carlos Hotel as soon as she decently could, after making her farewells to the Cameron brothers and their wives, making sure Buffie also had a ride home, and after fending off with smiles and gentle disclaimers a few more congratulations on her singing and good wishes for the future of the company.

She was feeling a tumult of emotions that was unusual for her as she jumped out of the car in front of her apartment house, thanking the Cowboy warmly and assuring him of her gratitude, but turning a deaf ear to his disappointed pleas that the evening was still young. It was, in fact, scarcely eleven, but Lee felt she had been through a year of psychological wear and tear. She was experiencing a mixture of ill-assorted reactions to all the glitter and excitement, stimulation from all the new faces and new acquaintances, pleasure at the unexpected adulation the genial crowd had accorded her, and then, darkening it all, that sudden plummeting drop in her spirits at the harsh accusation and bitter anger with which Ben Cameron had confronted her in the room back of the bandstand. She felt unfairly accused, misunderstood, what her Aunt Bess used to call "put upon."

She stepped inside her apartment, closed the door behind her, and leaned against it wearily, switching on the lights as she did so. Tired though she was, she knew she would find it hard to sleep tonight—her mind was still keyed-up, restless, wide-awake. Wired, Steve would have said. And suddenly the compact, cozy little apartment that she loved so well and in which she had always felt so safe and snug seemed too small to hold the inner explosions that she could feel growing in her. She needed—what? Openness, fresh air, room to move and to let her thoughts run free—an idea churned up suddenly and rose to the surface of her restless mind. Without giving her rational self a chance to review and then reject it as impulsive and foolish, she hurried to her bedroom and stripped off the green silk dress, tossing it on the bed and then kicking off her thin-strapped high-heeled sandals, not caring that one landed in a corner and one skidded under the bed. Hurriedly she pulled on jeans and the T-shirt Steve had presented to her one day. It said WW MUSIC—COUNTRY FOREVER across the front. Then she pulled on her old, worn Tony Lama boots, grabbed a denim jacket and her big soft shoulder bag, and went back out, turning off lights as she went.

She hurried to her parking space back of the apartment building, got into the car, and started it, thankful that she had filled the gas tank earlier. Putting sensible arguments behind her, she drove out of the parking area toward the first traffic light, where she turned left and headed toward the superhighway, the hundred-mile concrete ribbon that would lead her through the night to Sulphur Springs.

Aunt Bess Colder, Dub's sister, who was never surprised at anything, accepted her arrival at one in the morning without the blink of an eye. She had, in fact, not yet gone to bed herself but was wide awake and busy in her kitchen.

"Best time to cook, I always thought," she said to Lee, coming over to give her a hug and then hurrying back to stir the pot with a long wooden spoon. "Nobody to bother you, and it's cooler." She did not ask what had brought Lee there in the middle of the night. Prying questions were not Bess Colder's way.

"Don't you want to know why I came?" Lee smiled at her, putting down her bag and slipping out of her jacket.

"Figure you'll tell me when you want me to know." Aunt Bess was tall and wiry-looking. Her hair, only slightly faded from its coppery color that was so like Lee's, was cut short and looked a bit uneven. Lee suspected she still went at it with the kitchen shears rather than bothering with the beauty shop.

"What's that? It smells delicious." Lee approached the fragrant kettle.

"Baked beans for the church picnic tomorrow afternoon after services," Bess explained. "You're welcome to come along. You always used to like them."

"I'll see," Lee hedged. "I just felt the need for some fresh air and open space. Peace and quiet too."

"Well, not likely you'd find those at a church picnic," Bess admitted. "You can suit yourself." They stood together at the stove for a moment and Lee put an arm across the older woman's shoulders. "Your room's where it always was," Bess said briskly.

"Thanks, Aunt Bess," Lee whispered.

She slept late, then saw Aunt Bess off to church in the ranch's old station wagon, helping her load pots, baskets, and casseroles into it and then watching as Bess jammed a shapeless straw hat down over her uneven hair and went roaring down the dirt drive to the county road. Lee returned to the house, drank two cups of coffee in the plain country kitchen, and ate one of Bess's buttermilk biscuits. Then she went out to the barn and saddled her horse Misty—fourteen now but well cared for. "You could use some exercise, old girl," Lee told her, leading her out into the stable yard. She mounted lightly to the saddle and watched as the horse's ears went forward with surprise and interest at this unexpected happening. Lee turned her away from the barn and headed her toward the open pasture and the woods and hills beyond. The sun was rising, strong and hot, but a quick, young breeze was coming in from the west. Misty responded with all the pleasure of a three-year-old, kicking up her heels and then lengthening her stride. Her ears lay back and her mane streamed in the wind as they headed across the field, Lee holding tight with her legs, leaning forward now and then to whisper praise and encouragement, feeling all the knots, tensions, and anxieties unravel, loosen, melt away.

It was late afternoon before they returned. Bess was still not back and Lee guessed she was not likely to be, not for a while. Church picnics were one of life's greatest pleasures as far as Bess Colder was concerned. Lee gave Misty a long, loving rubdown, fed and watered her, then went into the house and located clean clothes, including a soft old denim shirt that she had left behind at the ranch. She bathed and changed quickly before heading for the kitchen to hunt for food. She was all at once surprisingly hungry. Big slices of baked ham piled lavishly on homemade bread took care of that, and Lee ate slowly, enjoying the peace and comfort of the place, the feel of the rough wooden table. When she had finished, she found a pencil that had been stuck into a glass with some teaspoons and wrote her aunt a brief note of thanks on a scrap of paper. A promise to come back soon and then: "I love you—Bonnie Lee." She washed her dishes, straightened the kitchen, and then walked slowly out to her car.

It was dark by the time she turned in at the parking lot by her apartment building, but she saw the car almost at once, its long, low shape parked in one of the empty spaces set aside for visitors. A heavy feeling of dread moved inside Lee, but she took a deep breath and parked in her own space, reminding herself that if she was not completely comfortable with the idea of seeing him again, at least she should be better able to handle the situation now. Some of the kinks and hangups and fears had worked out of her during her day in the country.

The Lincoln's door opened and she saw his long legs, then the rest of him as he got out and came over to her. He looked, in the pale illumination of the parking lot, drawn and tired. Lee, full of fresh air and the reassurance of home, experienced a moment's wild irrational longing to stroke the dark hair, to ease away the worry lines.

"Where the devil were you, anyway?" he demanded, his voice sharp with accusation, and all thoughts of tenderness fled Lee's mind. "Good evening to you too," she said with heavy sarcasm.

"Where were you?" he repeated.

"Riding an old horse over half of East Texas."

"I telephoned several times and then I decided to come over here—I was beginning to worry."

"Not about me, surely. Or should I be touched at the interest?" She reached for her handbag, opened the car door, and got out. Her hair still looked windblown and there was color in her cheeks. His eyes moved over her with a curious mixture of irritation and something else she could not read.

"I just couldn't figure out where you'd gone. I finally called Buffie to ask if she knew. Only she didn't. An old horse?" he asked with a scowl as though just now taking note of her answer.

She ignored the question. "Why on earth did it matter?"

"I was thinking about the recording session. There were things I wanted to ask you. I even went to the office."

Lee had locked the car and started to move away. She whirled around to face him. "You did what?"

"Well, I thought you might possibly have gone there—for some reason. Anyway, I wanted to—"

"That's not why you went there," she interrupted him, speaking slowly and icily. "You were checking up on me, weren't you? You thought I might have stolen the tape and left town. That's what you were afraid of, isn't it?"

"Certainly not." His mouth tightened angrily. "What I actually went there for was—"

"You really are something, you know that?" Lee exploded. "You don't trust anybody, do you?" She could feel herself trembling with rage and close to tears.

He said coldly, "I was about to say that I went there to make a cassette for Nikki, so that she could be working on the songs. It did occur to me in passing that you might have gone there."

"I don't appreciate having people track me down when I want to be alone for a few hours," she said with cold anger.

She saw a tightening at the corners of his mouth, saw his features move into stoniness.

"Please don't worry about it. I can assure you it won't happen again," he said tersely. "Believe me, your whereabouts are of no personal interest to me whatever."

She turned and walked away from him. By the time she reached the door and began fumbling for her key, her eyes were dimming over with tears, but even the surge of anger that had risen in her like a powerful tide did not quite smother the other thing—a lonely, desolate pain closing like a fist around her heart.

CHAPTER TEN

She had heard her father say it often enough. It had become a recurrent theme in her life. And it was the first thing she thought of when she woke up the next morning. "Well, look here, sugar. When things don't go right, or you have a setback, ain't anything you can do but pull your socks up and go at it again." It had been Dub's philosophy of life, and even though in the end it had failed him, it was still something he had wanted to instill in her. Surprisingly he had succeeded. As Lee got up and made coffee, showered, and dressed, she began going over her options, reviewing the possibilities.

One thing rose to the surface as paramount. If she wanted to stay with WW Music, if she wanted to be a part of it still—and anything else was inconceivable to her—then she would have to start learning to get along with Ben Cameron. Put distance between them, but get along. Her conscious mind accepted this sensible reasoning. Deep inside her where her heart did the dictating, a sharp and bitter pain kept reminding her that it would not be that easy. But if she put her mind to it, she could do it, she insisted to herself. And Nikki North herself would make it easier. She had obviously set her sights on Ben and he, equally obviously, was responding to her. There could be no doubt about what stage the affair had reached. The dreamy satisfied look in Nikki's eyes when they emerged from the elevator after two hours alone in the hotel suite had told Lee that.

Brushing out her coppery hair and applying lipstick lightly, Lee drew a deep breath to clear her head. For the immediate future, her job was to help get the new album off the ground. It wouldn't be easy, either emotionally or technically. But she was the one with the knowledge and experience, and much as she disapproved of the project, the decision was out of her hands. It was Ben Cameron's to make, and he had made it. Looking in the mirror, she saw the harsh twist that her mouth took at the thought, and quickly smoothed it away. If only she could smooth away that easily the stabbing pain inside her.

Firmly and decisively, she put all such thoughts away from her. Think about work, think about the problems to be solved, she ordered herself. She began to put them in order.

Ben said that he had given a cassette of Dub's songs to Nikki so that she could start learning them. But she would need more than that, Lee's common sense told her. First order of business would be to get Buffie or Jennifer to type up the lyrics so that Nikki could learn them properly. Then it might help if she were to give Nikki some pointers on Dub's style and approach to a song—go over the material with her. Lee was under no illusion that Nikki would welcome this kind of help. Her dislike of Lee after the unfortunate business of Tad Summers' column was something she did not even try to hide. And the singing episode at the reception had only made it worse. Still, she would make the offer, Lee decided, trying for the most tactful approach. Nikki and Joe Bud were doing a benefit shot at the San Carlos Hotel in a few days—all part of the promotion and publicity accompanying their move to Dallas. That would probably be the best hook on which to hang it. Mr. Cameron was worried that he'd given you too much work all at once, she could say. He wants me to smooth the way for you by giving you a hand with the new material. Shaky, but a possibility, she decided. Before leaving for the office she grabbed up the guitar case holding the beautiful Martin that Dub had given her and brought it along. She'd better keep it close to her for the time being, she decided; she might be needing it.

Next was the matter of backup musicians. There too she would have to supply some help. The Mother Lode was a good, steady band, but she thought they lacked the experience for this kind of work—laying down tracks on tape and following the relaxed, distinctive thread of Dub's singing. She would see if Bobby Clausen and his group were available. They were a first-rate studio band, experienced and capable. The drummer would be crucial, having to pick up the tempo from Dub and put it on tape behind him. Not an easy job. The drummer usually set the beat rather than followed it, but Bobby's drummer—what was his name?—Pete Something—was good. So was the steel man; she remembered him.

Her head full of plans, ideas, mental notations, Lee stepped into the office briskly an hour later. In the back of her mind a nagging small voice persisted in reminding her of a few unpleasant truths—that putting distance between Ben Cameron and her wouldn't be the easiest job in the world, what with seeing him every day and hearing his voice every time she moved in or out of her office. And getting along with him— that was not going to be a simple matter either. He had an arrogant, abrasive way about him that always managed to ruffle her into resistance. But she was determined to do it. To remain the correct, helpful employee, with all her enthusiasm directed toward the company and its future. And I can do it, she told herself firmly. If I try hard enough, I can do it.

"Morning, Jennifer. Morning, Buffie," she said cheerfully.

"Oh, Miss Colder, you were simply wonderful the other night," Jennifer said admiringly. "I mean your singing—we all loved it!"

"Thanks, Jennifer," Lee said, passing it off casually and realizing with a sense of shock that the blonde with Steve, the one in the strapless white dress, had been Jennifer. In the excitement of the moment, it had not even registered with her. Well, well. Steve's exploits were getting harder and harder to keep up with, she thought with amusement.

"We all loved it," Buffie added enthusiastically. "And wasn't it the loveliest party, Lee? I don't know when I've had such a good time."

"Oh, it certainly was," Lee agreed, knowing Buffie was finding it hard to get her feet on the ground again. "But back to work now, Buffie. Have you time to do a typing job for me?

Maybe Jennifer could give you a hand with it." She explained
what was needed and promised to run off a cassette quickly
that the two of them would be able to transcribe from. "And
would you look up Bobby Clausen's number for me, Jennifer?"
She spelled it for her. "It should be in the red book, the one
with all the special phone numbers. Too early to call him now,
I suppose. He probably had late-night jobs over the weekend.
I'll try around noon. Then when the lyrics are typed, I'd better
get in touch with Miss North and see about setting up an
appointment with her to run over the songs."

"Oh dear, my typing isn't too good," Buffie said doubtfully.

"Anything I can help with?" Doris, whose last name Lee had
not yet learned, came out of Ben's private office and glanced
around at the three of them. A plain, dumpy woman of thirty-
five or so who seemed to thrive on work, she radiated efficiency, which had probably accounted for Buffie's swift hiring
of her as Ben's private secretary.

"Just some song lyrics that need typing, Doris," Lee replied.
"Rather tricky—from a cassette—"

"Nonsense, I'll be glad to do it," Doris said with flat matter-
of-factness, and then could not resist adding, "It should be
done right."

Before she could turn back, a voice called out from behind
her, "Doris, I've misplaced those copyright forms Buffie
handed me. Have you seen—"

Lee felt her breath catch in a small, hot stab as she looked up
and saw Ben standing there framed in the doorway to his
office.

"Oh, good morning, Lee," he said as he saw her. His voice
was completely cool and normal, and only the tiniest flush of
color spreading up over his cheekbones revealed any feeling.
Even that, Lee thought, was only the betrayal of a slight embarrassment, nothing more.

"Good morning," she said quietly. "Just making arrangements for typing up the lyrics for Nikki—she'll be needing
them to learn the songs."

"Ah, I see. Fine. Good idea," he said, and hesitated only a moment before turning back and disappearing into his office.

Moments later in the jumble of the storeroom that nevertheless seemed to fall into its own kind of order, Lee threaded Dub's tape through the machine and set it for re-recording on a cassette. She walked to the one small window which opened onto a ventilating shaft and while the tape was spinning off silently, gazed out at blank walls.

"Enjoying the view?"

She whirled around at the sound of the voice behind her. Ben stood just inside the room, his deep blue eyes probing the distance between them, studying her, not smiling. He did not wait for an answer. "I wanted to thank you," he said, speaking quietly.

Lee was throbbingly aware of how her pulse started to race, how the hot blood started to surge through her veins. Maddening, in the face of the cool decisions she had made that morning. If I'm ever to do this thing, she told herself furiously, I must get it under control—the whole ridiculous set of responses that spring up when I'm with him.

"For what?" she said pleasantly, and her tone was a triumph of self-control.

"For taking hold, getting this recording thing under way. I know you don't approve of the idea, but I want you to know I appreciate your putting that to one side and taking over. I do need your experience, just as my brother Frederick said the other night. I still have a great deal to learn."

That was an opening a mile wide, she told herself ruefully—a place to insert the knife, to lash out with sarcasm. But what good would it all do? It would only keep this exhausting feud between them going in high gear. Better to dive down a harmless bypath. "I liked your brothers," she said brightly. "Frederick especially seemed to me a very warm and caring person."

"Oh, he is. They both are, actually, although Philip gives the impression of computerlike efficiency. He's not that way at all, really. He and Sondra have five kids and raise golden retrievers. You wouldn't think so, would you?"

She smiled in spite of herself, the picture was so out of keeping with what she had imagined. "I can't believe it," she said.

He crossed the room with slow steps. Behind them the tape whirred with a soft rustling sound.

"Lee. . . ."

Her eyes stayed on his face even though she willed them to look elsewhere. "Yes?"

"I hope we're still friends," he said hesitantly.

"Of course," she said, but even to her own ears it had an automatic sound, hollow and formal.

"I just wish we could go back," he said.

"Go back—to where?"

"You know, back to square one. Start over. I think we got off on the wrong foot somehow. All my fault, I'm sure, but I would like to try again."

She succeeded in lowering her eyes slightly, to a point just below his chin. "I don't think we can do that," she said slowly.

"Why not?"

She had become acutely aware of the fresh male scent of him, the warmth of his body's nearness to her. She concentrated on keeping her voice firm and unwavering.

"Because it would just be pretending. You can't really go back. Everything we said and did and thought is right there, isn't it?"

"We'll ignore it."

"But that's not possible, is it?" Her shoulders squared, her chin rose slightly as she looked at him. Her spine grew stiffer and straighter, although she did not realize it. "We have to be honest, don't we?"

"And the honest truth is that you dislike me, is that it?" Frost was creeping into his voice, turning the blue eyes cold.

"No, of course not," she said. "And it has nothing to do with liking or not liking anyway. It's a difference of opinion, that's all, about something to do with business. And where business decisions are to be made, you're the one to make them now. I recognize that, and I want to give the company my very best. If we just keep it that way, I'm sure we'll get along fine."

She saw his eyes glitter with sudden cold and in that moment she knew a wild longing to have his arms around her, to feel his lips come down crushingly on hers, until the rest of the world was eclipsed. The thought of that warm, moving mouth covering hers sent white heat into spinning skyrockets in Lee's head, sent spirals of longing and desire whirling into her body's deepest recesses. She could almost feel her body pressed against his—so close that curves and hollows, bone and muscle fused, melted, blended together, became one throbbing whole.

Behind them the faint buzz of the turning tape stopped with a click. The room was suddenly silent. *End of side one*—the words echoed in Lee's head. *Turn tape to record side two.* If only it were that easy, she thought achingly. If only life offered us that option, to start fresh as with a new tape, blank and untouched. But there were no such easy solutions in real life.

Hastily she turned away from him and went to turn the cassette. She did not trust herself to speak again. Even if she had wanted to, even if she could have thought of the right thing to say, she knew she could not have trusted her voice at that moment. Fumbling with the cartridge, she heard his long, angry stride as he crossed the room and slammed out.

When the lyric sheets had been neatly typed by the efficient Doris, Lee sent them to Nikki at the hotel by messenger. Later she called to offer help. She would be happy to run through them with Miss North if it would make it easier for her. She received a curt refusal from someone named Dolores, who was, it appeared, Nikki's maid-hairdresser, and who told her crisply that Miss North said she did not require help. Now that she had the typed lyric sheets and the cassette, she would be able to manage quite well on her own. When they were ready for her in the studio, she would appear, not before. Lee sighed and turned her attention to the matter of working on the tape.

It was a week of nonstop work, of rehearsals, appointments, arrangements, and run-throughs. It was harder, Lee observed to herself, than all the work she had done before when she had handled the plans for the reception. But at least this was something familiar, something known, something she felt confident she could do well. She was on her own ground here, and nothing was too much for her, no hours too long, no work too arduous. She succeeded in getting the backup band she wanted, and with them she went to the big new studio in Cambro Park and worked long hours at recording on separate tape tracks the music that would accompany Dub's singing. Nikki's voice would be the last to be added. When it was done, it would, she hoped earnestly, sound like a finished, cohesive product. Even as she winced inwardly at the word *product*, she knew that it fitted exactly. For what they were turning out was a salable item, not a record reflecting artistry and heart. All she could do at this point was monitor it carefully, demand the best from all the musicians, and hope that in the end the result would not do too much damage to Dub's memory. From the first it was difficult, however. Even the skilled musicians she had hired had trouble, and it was up to Lee to encourage, criticize, suggest.

"Maybe if we could just try the drums once more."

"It's damned tricky, Lee, trying to pick up his beat."

"I know, Bud. Let's just give it one more try. And wait with the steel, Bill. Let it slide in over the top in the break." Sometimes she would take her guitar out and play with them briefly to illustrate a point.

Patiently and with surprising good nature, the musicians went through take after take, with Ed Farraday in the big glassed-in room managing the controls.

"How does it sound now, Lee? Shall I bring the guitars up a little more?"

"I don't think so, Ed. We've got to keep the voices up front— Dub's, and then we still have to add Nikki's later."

Each night when Lee returned to her apartment, she had strength enough only to shower and fall into bed, exhausted.

And if there was one thing out of it all to be grateful for, she told herself ruefully, it was that there was very little room in her head for thoughts of Ben Cameron right now. That's one problem I don't need at this point, she thought.

Through all the days of working on the background music, coaxing the band into one more take, placating tempers and egos, the matter of Nikki and her contribution to the record was a dark cloud of dread on the horizon. Lee knew the issue had to be faced soon. At last she decided there was no point in delaying any longer.

"We've put down the band tracks and we have the original tape well integrated with them," she told Ben at the end of the week. "Let's get Nikki into the studio now and see how she sounds with the rest."

She had made no special effort to avoid him during the week, but had tried to act as businesslike and practical as possible whenever she did see him. Because she had stayed so busy, it had not been difficult, yet she was conscious every time she was with him of tight-lipped withdrawal on his part, of coldness and a sense of distance between them.

"All right," he agreed crisply. "Tomorrow?"

"Fine. Will you bring her? That is, to offer encouragement and so on."

"I'll be glad to bring her, of course, but I doubt if she'll need encouragement. Nikki's a professional. I'm sure she'll do fine."

"Yes, of course."

It was early afternoon by the time Nikki appeared the next day, radiant and smiling, holding tight to Ben's arm. Joe Bud Garrett was already in the studio, sitting with Lee. "I'm not really needed, of course," he had said good-naturedly. "This show's all Nikki's. But you never know, I might be able to help here and there."

"I'm glad you came," Lee said honestly. Somehow she always felt she had a friend present with Joe Bud around.

Nikki was talking animatedly as she came into the big main room, looking up into Ben's face and punctuating her remarks with small smiles and pouts and not letting go his arm. She was wearing tight-fitting jeans and a hot pink off-the-shoulder blouse. Her look glanced off Lee, barely touching. Her hello was so brief and casual that Lee's spirits, which she had been keeping up with dogged optimism, went plummeting. This was not going to be easy, she thought. Nikki's first words ominously bore out her worst fears.

"I hope this isn't going to take long," Nikki said airily.

It was three in the afternoon when Nikki slipped the headphones on over her frosted curls to listen to the tape on which Lee had been working so hard all week—Dub Colder's voice and guitar with the new background music filled in by the studio band.

"Let me just run through it once to get all the words in the right places," Nikki said.

"Sure," Ben agreed pleasantly. "We'll tape everything, but remember, it's just a demo session, a chance for us to hear how it all sounds—right, Ed?" He turned to the engineer, who had joined them. "We'll keep playing back and listening, and of course, you never know, we might get lucky. One of the takes might turn out to be great, in which case our work here will be finished."

"Piece of cake," Nikki twinkled at him.

It took no more than twenty minutes for Lee to realize that they were in deep trouble. It took another hour for tact, flattery, and persuasion to convince Nikki that she needed help. In the end it was Joe Bud Garrett who, pleading with her in his soft country voice, managed to get her to accept it.

"Best thing to do, honey, to get over this tricky part, would be to let Lee here work it out with you. It's her daddy's music and she knows his style real well, see."

Nikki's face had darkened with an angry flush. Her hair was beginning to rumple and to stick out in disheveled strands. "I don't see why I should be struggling like this to get along with someone else's style—I've got my own style!"

"Sure you do, baby. And soon as this is wrapped up, you'll be right back with it. It's just a one-shot deal, and a million-dollar piece of publicity for you. You don't want to pass that up, do you?"

Nikki made an impatient movement of her head and consulted a tiny diamond-set watch on her wrist. "I really do want to get out of here," she said with irritation. "And I don't want to use my voice too much. We have that benefit show to do tonight and I still have to have my hair done and rest for a while—oh, all right," she said, giving Lee a resentful glance.

Joe Bud made a beckoning motion, and Lee got up from where she had been sitting and joined them, bringing her guitar with her. Her eyes went briefly to the control room where Ben had gone to sit with Ed Farraday and listen to the playback. For a moment their glances met; then he looked away. Lee went and perched on a stool beside Nikki.

"Let's take the headphones off for now," she suggested. "Forget about the mike and everything else. Let's just run over that first song together. I'll show you how the harmony goes. You start out all right, you see, but then you seem to wind up singing in unison with Dub's voice. I know it's tricky, but perhaps if I show you the notes . . ."

They went through it twice. Ben had come out of the control room and was standing on the sidelines with Joe Bud. Lee, feeling his presence, knowing he was there, made a special effort to concentrate on the task at hand, coaxing, wheedling, encouraging a performance out of Nikki as once again the singer put the headphones on to try a run-through.

"Very good, Nikki," Ben said during the pause after they had finished. "Much better, don't you think, Lee?"

"Yes, much," Lee said politely, but knowing the truth would have to be faced sooner or later. Nikki was not going to turn out a good take this afternoon, and it was highly doubtful if even a second session would produce one. She was, quite simply, out of her depth. Still, Lee felt she had to keep trying.

"Now on this next song, if you could take it up a little, Nikki. Just a bit higher," Lee coaxed. "And try to modulate along with him on this phrase . . . no, more like this . . . that's it.

Now be sure to hang onto your harmony here, but keep it very tight, over the top, and soft, as a sort of background."

Nikki's composure went shattering.

"What the hell do you mean—'background'?" she shouted, snatching off the headphones and throwing them to the floor. "I don't sing background—not for anyone!"

Lee gave her a startled look, and in a sudden protective gesture swung the gleaming Martin out of Nikki's reach. Ben and Joe Bud were both on their feet, and the silence in the studio echoed Nikki's strident tones like an aftermath of glass shattering. Ben came forward at once and said in smoothly placating tones, "Absolutely not, Nikki. I'm sure Lee didn't mean that quite as it sounded. Besides, we've worked much too long for today. Let's call it a wrap and get you back to the hotel. After the show tonight we'll give you the weekend off and then come back to this Monday. I'm sure we can finish it easily once you've had a chance to rest up."

Nikki, breathing rapidly, nostrils flaring, eyes snapping fire, looked every inch a star, although a somewhat disheveled one, as she allowed herself to be led out of the studio by Ben. Joe Bud Garrett walked with them as far as the door, then said a few private words to Ben and returned to where Lee was putting her guitar back in its case. For a moment he stood watching her, arms folded in front of him, an amused grin creasing his face.

"Know what we're going to do now, sugar?" he said softly.

Lee shook her head, feeling all at once wretched as a heavy, oppressive sense of failure settled down over her like a black cloud. She had handled it badly, been too brusque with Nikki, forgotten the kid-glove approach in her concentration on the music and its demands. It was her fault, and there was no tactful way to undo it.

"Hey, are you listening to me? I just told the boss man you deserved a reward for the day you put in. I'm taking you out to dinner. Come on, come on, let's get moving."

Lee's head had come up in startled response as she tried to focus on what he was saying. "Dinner?" she echoed.

"No excuses now. Actually, I think you deserve a medal, but dinner's going to have to do. Besides, I want to show off my new car."

Lee shook her hair back and protested, "But you and Nikki have a show to do later at the hotel. You'll want to get ready for it—"

"Now that's a *real* piece of cake," he said. "All I have to do is put on a clean shirt and tune my guitar."

She looked at him for a moment. His broad grin, his infectious good humor, acted on her like a tonic. You could not be around Joe Bud Garrett long, she thought, without falling in with his mood. "All right," she agreed. She glanced toward the control room. "Let's just say goodbye to Ed."

They opened the door to the control room where the engineer, looking troubled, was listening to one of the takes over the large speakers. He saw them and raised his shoulders in a slight, futile gesture. Then his eyes scanned the board and all the vast array of buttons, knobs, and controls.

"This board will do a lot of things," he said wearily. "I just can't get it to sing harmony."

CHAPTER ELEVEN

Lee had to admit to herself that it was pleasant having dinner with Joe Bud Garrett. The small, exclusive restaurant where he took her was full of diners who were obviously sophisticated, worldly, not easily impressed. Yet in spite of that several of them managed to find their way to him and to shake his hand. Some of the women even asked for his autograph on a menu. "Just to take home to the kids," one said, but Lee knew quite well it was not for the kids. Joe Bud had a way of affecting women with his slow smile, his down-home speech, and men did not resent it, but seemed to like him equally well. His face had laugh lines and sun lines. "Like ten miles of bad road," she had heard him say. Yet it was all part of what had made him a success, along with his singing. She could see now that the smile he gave to strangers was an automatic response, a habit cultivated over the years. And he was certainly not the down-home country boy he appeared to be at first acquaintance. He was a seasoned pro who knew what effect he was creating every minute, yet it was impossible to resent him. And perhaps, Lee suspected, the public image was not so different after all from the private person underneath. A core of kindness and good humor remained there, even with all the success. Painfully Lee wished that Nikki North had an ounce or two of it. She could not imagine how they would ever finish the recording even after Nikki had had a weekend to recover.

Joe Bud, seating himself after having autographed a menu for a well-upholstered, silver-haired woman, seemed to glimpse her thoughts. "It's going to be all right, honey," he assured her, patting her hand. "Nikki flares up, but she simmers down just as fast. The thing is, she's not as sure of herself as she'd like the world to believe."

Lee realized that she had already guessed this. "I'm afraid I just don't know how to approach her," she said worriedly. "I don't know the right way to handle her."

"Natural enough," he shrugged. "You're thinking about the music and she's thinking about her own image." The waiter came and took their order, brought the bottle of white wine Joe Bud had requested, and left them. Joe Bud said thoughtfully, "She's not the greatest singer in the world, you know."

Lee studied his face curiously over the rim of her wineglass as she took a slow sip. "Then if you don't mind my asking, why—" She broke off, finding the question too difficult to phrase tactfully. Again he was ahead of her.

"Why did I team up with her?" He grinned quite openly. "Good for both of us, I suppose. She's decorative and she has a certain appeal with audiences. It's a matter of looks and personality rather than talent, of course, but I have enough experience to carry it off for both of us. And at this stage of my career it hasn't done me any harm, appearing with her. It's been a kind of revival for me, a second wind. And she's learned a lot along the way, so I feel I've helped her too. She's getting there—slowly. I mean, she'll never be a first-rate singer. I suspect she knows that. But she'll have herself a career of sorts." He paused and added thoughtfully, "Big success isn't always a matter of big talent, honey."

"I'm afraid I ruffle her terribly," Lee said.

"She'll get over it. Right now she's probably soaking in a hot tub and getting ready for the show tonight at the hotel. I don't imagine she's even thinking about what happened at the studio. And if she's managed to coax the big boss man into the tub with her, she's probably happier than a hound dog on a possum hunt." He caught Lee's startled expression and added, "Oops, sorry—I think I said the wrong thing there."

Lee looked away quickly as some well-dressed new arrivals entered and provided a distraction. She was astonished herself at how his flippant remark had stabbed at her. By the time she returned to him, however her expression was composed, revealing nothing.

"It's all right," she said quietly. "There's nothing between Ben Cameron and me." Then, before he could speculate further, she hurried on, "Actually I thought perhaps you and Nikki had some sort of—you know, that the two of you . . ."

Joe Bud put his head back and laughed heartily. "Oh Lord no. Nothing there. Although I will admit that just at first we had a little go-around. It was how she attracted my notice in the first place. She was in Nashville haunting the producers' offices. Miss Something-or-Other."

"Miss Metroplex," Lee supplied.

"That's right," he grinned. "And I will say she knew how to get your attention. But now it's strictly business, and better that way. As I say, it's worked out well for both of us. And sugar, don't take me too seriously about the hot tub. I don't think our man Ben is the type, actually."

"I'm afraid I don't really know what type our man Ben is," Lee said, looking down at her glass. More and more, she realized, that was coming to be the truth.

With the tact that never seemed to desert him, Joe Bud managed a change of subject.

"You want to know what I kept thinking this afternoon, sugar?" he asked.

Her head came up. "What?"

The question hung in the air as the waiter returned with their order and served them, moving quietly around to adjust plates and glasses, then gliding away.

"I was thinking what a whale of a record that could be if you were to do the singing with your daddy."

Lee smiled at him. "Like an old movie I was watching on television the other night," she said. "Understudy waiting in the wings, star breaks a leg: her big chance."

"Well, in a way. We won't wish a broken leg on Nikki, but still . . ." He paused as he saw Lee shaking her head.

"You're very sweet to say it," Lee said slowly. "And I know you mean it. Only that's not what the record needs. Dub never

needed anybody singing with him. Oh, we used to sing together at home, sure. But his records were always just him.
And it was that sound—I guess maybe it was a lonesome sound
—that was just his. That's what people loved." She looked him
squarely in the eyes. "What that record needs, really, is to be
left alone."

He considered it, eyes crinkled up and studying her. "Well,
you might be right. But I don't think that's likely to happen. I
mean, I get the feeling that when Ben Cameron gets an idea in
his head, he really digs in."

She nodded, but could not resist a small, wry smile. "Like a
hound dog on a possum hunt?"

"Maybe. Or maybe more like a Texas mule with his mind
made up."

As they left the restaurant, a few more autograph seekers
waylaid them, but Lee did not mind. It was rather flattering
and exciting, in a way, to be with someone so sought after, and
Joe Bud was protectively solicitous of her—quick to take her
elbow, to guide her through the crowd. The parking attendant
brought Joe Bud's shiny new white Seville up with a flourish,
grinning from ear to ear.

Lee said quickly, in a low voice, "Look, you don't have to
bother to take me home, Joe Bud; I can get a cab. And I don't
want to make you late. You still have a show to do."

"The show's not till eleven," he reassured her. "Plenty of
time. Anyway, I'm not taking you home. We still have a party
ahead of us."

"A party!" Lee echoed, staring at him in bewilderment.

"Sure. In that suite that the Cameron brothers maintain way
up at the top of the hotel. It'll be just a small affair this time—
not a big bash like the other night. A few reporters, I guess, but
not a big deal. A reception and warmup for the benefit, all in
the name of good publicity."

The thought of seeing Ben again made Lee's heart race like
a bird beating its wings against her ribs, yet filled her with
dread at the same moment. "Oh, I'm not dressed for a party,
Joe Bud. I mean, really, I'd rather not. . . ."

Joe Bud regarded her for a moment, observing the way the cool night breeze pressed the silky blue dress against her slender curves and riffled the bright hair that fell to her shoulders.

"Hey, sugar," he said softly. "If anybody could look better than you do right this minute, I'd sure like to know how. Come on, it'll do you good." He took her elbow and helped her into the car, then went around to the driver's side. "Anyway, you said you wanted to do everything you could to bring off this session. This'll be a little fence mending. Nikki's going to be in a good mood with all the attention, everybody taking her picture—you and she ought to hit it off fine now."

Privately Lee had her doubts about this, yet she had learned that Joe Bud's plain-speaking observations were often grounded in truth, so she made no more objections as they drove off toward Cambro Park and the San Carlos Hotel. On the way she even managed to make complimentary comments about the car, which was still extravagantly new and leather-smelling, and to force her mind firmly away from the thought that it was in that same luxury suite that Ben and Nikki had spent those two intimate hours the other evening.

The Cameron brothers' company suite in the San Carlos was already crowded when they got there, smoke-filled and buzzing with conversation. Lee could see that it had been decorated in the same color scheme of green and peach that she had observed downstairs in the lobby and which seemed to carry throughout the hotel. There was a big modular couch upholstered in peach-colored wool, there were sea-green upholstered chairs done in the shape of seashells. There was a huge glass-topped coffee table resting on a geometric-patterned dhurrie rug that had been laid over the carpeting. Except for an occasional chrome floor lamp, there was no illumination except from recessed ceiling fixtures and concealed lighting strips. A sleek dining table with modern chairs stood alone at one end—for private conference dinners, Lee guessed. Several paintings provided horizontal slashes of color on the pale walls.

As Lee and Joe Bud entered, flashbulbs were making little

bright stabs in the subtle lighting of the room. Nikki was in the center of a cluster of reporters once more, and others were crowded on the outer fringe. Some of them Lee recognized, others were vaguely familiar. In the new, more vibrant reincarnation of WW Music, she was becoming accustomed to this crowd, a retinue of half acquaintances, of faces almost recognized. Opportunism had replaced friendship, promotion and public relations seemed to have taken over from talent, she thought. Then at once she put such thoughts behind her, dismissing them impatiently. She had never had a good head for the business end of the music business, she thought. It was not fair to resent someone who had. She became aware of a tall form a few paces behind Nikki and lifted her eyes to Ben Cameron's face.

At almost the same moment his blue eyes, combing the room in an idle way as though hiding boredom, locked with Lee's, and for the space of an instant the look between them held, taut and stretched, vibrating like a thin steel wire. Then, quite unexpectedly, he smiled. The smile, more startling to Lee than a scowl would have been, sent tremors fingering down her spine and invading her midsection. Without willing herself to, she felt herself smiling back. In an instant he was pushing through the crowd to her side.

"Lee! I'm so glad you came." His voice held such open, undisguised pleasure that once again Lee was struck with how much he still remained a stranger to her, how little she really knew him.

"She held out against it, but I took and hauled her here," Joe Bud said in his best country style.

"I'm glad you did," Ben said warmly, and added, looking down at her, "I'd have invited you myself, only somehow I didn't think you'd come."

The blue of his eyes seemed to seize her and hold her against her will. "I really didn't mean to—that is, I didn't want to come bursting in this way."

"Hey, Madam Vice President, you know you're always welcome." It was a bantering voice, but there was gentleness in his expression, and a great warmth of tenderness in the look he was giving her. *Couldn't we go back to square one*, he had asked her. And she had said no. But might it be possible? Was there even a chance?

Joe Bud, looking from one to the other with a kind of dry humor, said, "I believe now's the time for me to change my shirt."

Ben's eyebrows went up in surprise. "Change your what?"

"Private joke," Joe Bud said, and leaned over to kiss Lee's cheek lightly. "Had a great time, sugar. See you later."

"Thanks, Joe Bud. I had a great time too," she said hastily.

"Don't miss the show now, you hear?" he said over his shoulder as he moved off. Lee and Ben looked at each other again, but now that they were alone, she felt a curious, churning discomfort, as though she could not think of a thing to say to him.

"This is a beautiful suite," she said tentatively.

He nodded. "Did you have a pleasant dinner?"

"Oh yes. Very nice. Where's the benefit to be held?"

"Downstairs in one of those big dining rooms. Federated Charities of Greater Dallas or some such thing—they made all the arrangements."

"Sounds like very good public relations."

"Yes." There was a long, empty pause, and then he said, "Would you like to see the rest of the apartment?"

It was like wading through deep water, Lee thought. Why couldn't they simply talk together like two ordinary acquaintances? Almost at once her own reasoning supplied the answer. Because nothing about their relationship was ordinary. It hadn't been from the very first moment they met. They had rubbed each other the wrong way, yet there had been through it all that strong, steely thread of physical attraction, pulling them inexorably toward each other. Or had that been mostly on her part, something she had only wished he might return? Certainly he had turned quickly enough to Nikki North—and right here in these very rooms. A sharp, twisting pain turned inside Lee at the thought. She tried to keep her voice even, so that it did not betray her.

"I'd like very much to see it," she said politely.

He took her elbow and guided her through the crowd of milling guests, smiling at this one and that but not stopping to speak to anyone. He pointed out the paintings on the wall. "The artist is up-and-coming, they tell me. And I guess you could say there's a certain vigor there . . ." His voice trailed off doubtfully.

"Vigor yes, heart no," she supplied, and they both laughed.

"Well, perhaps in corporate decor, one serves as well as the other."

"And maybe in corporate life in general?" she asked.

His grip on her elbow tightened perceptibly. "No, I don't think I'd agree with that." He moved in the direction of a small kitchen, narrow and galley-style, with a hardwood floor. "You see—all the amenities, only I don't imagine we'll ever use it."

"I can't exactly picture cooking up a mess of chili in it. Not if you planned on turning around more than once or twice."

There was a sudden silence between them as they remembered the night they had eaten chili in her small apartment and the storm that had pounded outside had been less furious than the passion they had both felt.

"Dining area over there, I guess you saw that," he said quickly.

"Yes, very striking."

"Now, over on this side"—he flung a door open—"the bedroom."

A huge king-sized, custom-made bed rested on a platform. The same peach and sea-green prevailed, only in this room the walls had been upholstered in what looked like a soft silken fabric with a muted sheen. A long platform extended at both sides of the headboard to form seating. Lights were soft, indirect.

"For visiting executives?" Lee asked in a voice that had grown suddenly small. All she could see was Nikki, with her little soft hands, her mouth in its appealing pout; Nikki, who knew exactly what she wanted and how to get it.

"Yes, of course." His own voice was noncommittal.

"Well, it's all simply stunning," Lee said, turning away hastily and heading back toward the crowded living room.

"Glad you approve."

They moved back among the others and did not speak again, but Lee could feel the slow, rhythmic pounding of her heart, deep and booming so that it almost seemed to her everyone in the room could hear it too. Pounding, pounding, with every step she took at his side.

Joe Bud had been right about Nikki. The center of attention in a black strapless gown, glittering with sequins, she was in an effusive, happy mood, the session in the studio quite forgotten. When she saw Lee, she said in a high, artificial voice, "Ah, here she is, the company slave driver. Lee darling, are you going to punish me and send me off to bed?"

Lee, recognizing the mood for what it was, purely temporary and for the benefit of outsiders, was quite willing to fall in with it.

"Not at all, Nikki. You've got a show to do. But just wait until next week!"

"Oh, she's a complete tyrant when it comes to work!" Nikki bubbled to the nearest reporter. "I'm absolutely terrified of her!"

Lee tried to manage a smile that would not show the bitter cynicism she was feeling. She had no knack when it came to the small deceits, the artificiality of situations like this, and she knew it.

Someone came up and spoke to Ben, pulling him aside and engaging him in some urgent question-and-answer conversation. He glanced at her with raised eyebrows and a helpless look, and she smiled back to indicate her understanding. The crowd seemed to close around her as people called out pleasantries, caught her arm, and started conversations that were as quickly broken off.

"Very exciting night, isn't it, Lee?"

"Just the kind of thing Dallas has been needing. . . ."

"Doesn't Nikki look like a million dollars?"

"Well, she's certainly a million-dollar property for WW Music. . . ."

"The thing about this Cambro outfit is, everything they touch seems to boom. . . ."

"Oh sure, the two brothers in Chicago, they're smart all right, but this fellow Ben's the one who's got the golden touch, I hear. . . ."

Then at last Joe Bud returned, resplendent in a silver Western-style shirt, fringe bobbing and catching the light, calling out, "Time to be moving downstairs, folks—show time!"

Nikki rolled her eyes upward in mock-panic. "Oh—hold my hand, somebody! I've suddenly got stage fright! Ben? Where's Ben?"

Spotting him across the room, she pushed toward him and seized his arm. Lee saw him bend down and speak to her—offering reassurance, it seemed—then escort her to the door. Others followed after them, and in the general movement to leave, Ben detached himself from her hold. "You'll be fine, Nikki; run along now." The words drifted back to Lee through the smoky, noisy room. Then Nikki was gone and he was seeing the others out. "Wonderful to see you. So glad you could come. Yes, I'll be right along. Get yourselves a good table now. Great, glad you could make it. . . ."

Incredibly, then, the huge room was quiet. Lee had moved over to the big window wall that faced toward the lights of downtown Dallas. She stood there, half turned away from the room. Out of the corner of her eye she saw a white-coated waiter start to put empty glasses on a tray, then saw Ben Cameron move to speak to him quietly. The waiter nodded and went out. She took a deep breath and turned brightly.

"Well, hadn't we better—"

At the same moment he said, "You haven't even had—"

Their words mingling, both of them laughed outright.

"You first," Lee said.

"I was only going to say that you haven't even had any champagne. How about having some now?"

"Well, what *I* was going to say was, hadn't we better get downstairs in a hurry if we want to see the show?"

He paused and pretended to consider it. "I'd say let's give priority to the matter of the champagne."

Lee felt her heart turning over, her whole body turning weak. Just being alone in a room with him can do that to me, she thought despairingly. But she kept her voice bright and offhand as she answered. "Oh, I really don't think—goodness, I've never had so much champagne in my whole life as this past week."

"Then surely one more glass won't make a difference," he said with authority, and found two fresh tulip glasses on a tray. He poured for both of them and handed her one. "Now we can have a private toast. What shall we drink to?"

"Oh—success of course," she said quickly.

His eyes did not leave her face. "And to us?"

She chose to misunderstand him deliberately. "Yes, of course. All of us."

The probing blue flame of light in his eyes flickered and narrowed but stayed fixed on her.

"You didn't really want to come here tonight, did you?"

She took a small sip and put the glass down. "What makes you say that?"

"Joe Bud's a pretty frank fellow. He indicated it took some persuasion."

"It's just that I was tired," she hedged. "It was a long day."

"I didn't thank you for that—for all your work in the studio."

"There wasn't any need. We all want to make a good record, don't we?"

"Yes, of course. And we're going to. I'm sure by next week all the kinks will be worked out."

She did not reply, but turned to the window again. She was conscious of his measured breathing close behind her. In a low voice he said, "Was there another reason why you didn't want to come here? Something more personal?"

A shudder passed through her slender frame. However much she wanted to blot the picture out, it kept recurring in her mind—clear and vivid. Nikki in that huge silken bed, languid and inviting. Nikki, who had long ago mastered every cunning sexual ploy for attracting men. Yet Lee's pride would not let her put it into words; she refused to let him know how much it had hurt her. At last he said it for her.

"Are you thinking about the other day when I was up here with Nikki—before the reception?" She did not answer. "Lee! You can't believe that—good Lord, I'm not interested in Nikki."

Something leaped joyfully inside her. She longed to be sensible and rational, above all, skeptical, but the joy was there nevertheless. It *could* be true, her heart sang. She turned to face him, all pretense forgotten.

"But when you came down in the elevator, the two of you looked so—so in love."

"Lee," he said softly, and reached up to touch her hair. "Don't you know Nikki's a great little actress? It was exactly what she wanted you to think. And if you saw anything in my expression that looked like love—well, it was your imagination at work, that's all."

Her heart singing, Lee whirled around again, not wanting him to see the sudden flush of happiness that she knew was in her face. "The view from here is really quite spectacular."

She heard the small clink as he set his own glass down. She felt his nearness as he came up behind her, caught that fresh, masculine scent she had noticed when she first met him. Then his hands were on her shoulders, lightly.

"Quite spectacular from here too," he said huskily, and she could feel his lips on her hair as he bent over her.

It was the moment she had been dreading, the moment she had known, somehow, lay somewhere in the future waiting for her. It was a moment of decision, a moment for firmness and strength. She had no wish to start the whole cycle of rapture and letdown, one following the other endlessly, and that was all it could ever be with Ben Cameron. She knew it.

"Isn't it time for the show?" she said lightly, but even to her own ears her voice had a hollow ring. "Shouldn't we be going?"

"I was wondering," he said, and the hands on her shoulders turned her toward him, "if we might skip the show."

Now there was no escaping the look in his eyes, the passionate tenderness, the forcefulness, the insistence. And in the deepest part of her being, Lee could feel all the same things crying out in answer. What good was her decision then to be strong, to resist, to stay aloof? How could she pretend indifference and coolness when her whole body felt ready to burst into flame? She was consumed with longing for him. She had wanted him always, she thought dizzily, from that first moment that he had confronted her in the office. She had wanted him that night in her apartment; she wanted him still, even as she tried to pretend otherwise.

"Do you really think—" she whispered.

But her words were stifled, cut short by his lips covering hers. His arms slid around her, moved down her back, pressed her to him. Hungrily Lee arched her body closer to his. His lips moved across her mouth, down to the hollow of her throat. His strong arms lifted her as if she were weightless and carried her into the bedroom.

Now, her resistance gone, her rational arguments silenced, Lee gave herself over to the dictates of the senses and to the wonder of their two bodies that could give and receive pleasure as if they had been destined for it from the beginning. Ecstasy moved along her arms and legs, trembled in her lips, throbbed in her breasts. Surprise that he could know her so well started rapture bursting inside her. She was surprised even at herself that she could respond, not holding back. But mostly she felt the shock of a knowledge that was astonishing to her—that their bodies could become one, all in an instant. The very wonder of it overwhelmed her, made her give back the same hot passion that he offered her, flaming and pulsing, insistent and demanding. Time lost all meaning to her; the future was something formless and shadowed—for now it did not exist. There was only this moment, and the close, warm intimacy of the bed where they lay.

Waking from sleep, drowsy and peaceful, Lee felt his arm thrown across her body. She stirred slightly and his arms tightened around her. He murmured her name in a low voice husky with sleep, pulled her close, and kissed her softly. Warm and suffused with love, safe in the circle of his arms, Lee slept again.

CHAPTER TWELVE

She had heard the pounding of the shower and now she could hear his soft footsteps coming up behind her in the tiny kitchen.

"I was wrong," she said. "You *can* turn around in this thing. I've done it twice already. And look, I've even found coffee." She held up the can to show him just as he circled her waist with both arms and turned her to face him.

"Room in here for me too?" he asked, and pulled her close to plant a long, soft kiss on her lips.

"Oh, careful, the lid's not on!" she laughed, and balanced the coffee can precariously over her head.

"It certainly isn't," he breathed close to her ear, and with one hand took the can from her and placed it on the counter.

"I've already put the water in, all you have to do is press the switch to turn it on," she said, nodding her head toward the automatic coffee maker.

"Just what I had in mind," he murmured, grinning and deliberately misunderstanding her.

"This kitchen really wasn't built for two," she observed. Her hands free, she slid them both around his waist and leaned her head against his bare chest. He had slipped into his trousers but was shirtless, and some dampness from the shower still clung to his skin. Lee had put on a soft shortie robe she had found hanging in the closet. She was barefooted, her red-gold hair hanging in a tousled mass around her shoulders.

"I'm sure this wasn't what Cambro intended this suite to be used for. I mean, it's for visiting executives, isn't it?" she asked, tipping her head up to scan his face lovingly. She felt, this morning, breathless with love, suffused with it, blissfully smothered in it. Since waking and seeing his dark, sleep-mussed hair on the pillow beside her, she had felt as if she were dream-walking. The lush carpets of the San Carlos became clouds. Looking out of the high windows, she seemed to see a personal view of heaven. What an absolutely ridiculous notion, she told herself, but she did not care. Have I ever been this happy before? she had asked herself, but knew she had not.

He was looking down at her and smiling with so much tenderness that her heart began pounding again. "Well, we're that, aren't we? Visiting executives?"

"If you stretch a point, I guess so," she admitted, returning the smile.

"Then let's make use of it, by all means."

"Yes—let's," she agreed as his mouth came down to cover hers again, but by now the pounding of her heart had grown so loud she was not sure he heard her.

They had their coffee in stylish, formal grandeur at the big dining table at one end of the room, laughing at their own bare feet and unkempt appearance.

"But really, we'd better dress and look respectable," she said. "Room service may be appearing any minute to clean all this up." She glanced around at the remains of the party—glasses, plates, and ashtrays scattered around the luxurious suite.

He shook his head. "I told them we'd call them when we needed them," he said.

She gave him a reproving look. "You had this planned all along."

His eyes sparkled. "From the moment I saw you come in that door with Joe Bud," he admitted. "Or even before. I guess from the first moment I saw you with your head stuck under that big desk." Gently he took her hand and pulled her to him so that she was sitting on his lap. "I love you, Bonnie Lee Colder," he whispered.

Both her arms were around his neck and for a long moment she scanned his features, looking deep into his eyes. Now the sharp, darting flames she had seen before were softened to a warm and tender glow. She longed to believe him; indeed at this moment she did believe him. And what in all the world matters except this moment? she asked herself.

"I'm afraid maybe I love you too," she whispered back.

"Afraid?" He drew back slightly and one dark eyebrow shot up.

"No," she corrected herself. "Not afraid. Not afraid of anything today." She let her head drop and rest in the hollow of his shoulder. His arms held her protectively against him.

"How would you like to spend the day in Chicago?" he asked abruptly.

Her head came up. "Chicago! What on earth—"

"I have to fly up there in the company plane, that's all. A nuisance, but I have to see Frederick and Philip about some stock transfers, sign some papers that Philip's been fussing about, take care of a few items of business that aren't related to WW Music, things I still have to keep an eye on. You could come along for the ride, enjoy a bit of northern spring, meet my numerous nieces and nephews."

"Oh, it sounds wonderful," she said, and hesitated. "But actually, do you know, I think I need this weekend."

"Need it?"

"Yes. Need it for myself. To think about what's happened, to be alone, to wander around and do a little singing with no one to hear."

He looked deep into her eyes. "What a funny little thing you are," he said softly. "I don't know how I can bear to be without you for a day."

"You'll live, I promise," she teased. "When are you coming back?"

"Tomorrow afternoon. I'll be at your apartment by six. Any more of that chili in the freezer?"

"Probably. Or steaks, anyway."

"Well then, be ready. Six o'clock now."

"All right. But I'd better shower and get out of here. You'll want to get started."

"I could lend a hand with that."

"With what?"

"That shower of yours."

She looked into his eyes, put both hands behind his head, and brought it down close so that she could kiss him.

"I hoped you were going to offer," she murmured.

Several times during the next twenty-four hours she reproached herself for not having gone with him to Chicago. Longing for his actual physical presence became an ache as the hours went by. Yet on another level she was glad for the solitude. So much that was wonderful had happened so fast that she felt she needed the time to absorb it, to make herself believe it was real.

She spent the next day walking, listening to her favorite records—everything from Bach to bluegrass—and then, her energy ready to burst its seams, cleaning house. It was during the cleaning that she did her own singing. Old songs and new ones, happy melodies and sad ones. Only today even the sad ones took on a lilt. By five o'clock the little apartment was spotless and glowing, two steaks were defrosting on the kitchen counter and a salad was in the refrigerator ready for tossing. She set the table with homespun place mats, fat white candles, and earth-toned plates. White wine was chilling, red wine was at room temperature, so they would have a choice. Satisfied that there was no more to be done, she went and showered and slipped into pale yellow slacks and a soft silk shirt. When she returned to the living room it was five forty-five. He had said six o'clock. And of course he might be early. Perhaps any minute now. She sat on the couch and picked up a magazine, turning the pages without seeing anything except a mélange of colors from the bright advertisements. She put it down and picked up a book. The words jumbled together madly. Her own happiness was so overwhelming that it would not admit another thought today. Concentration on anything but him was out of the question.

Six o'clock came and went. She tried to keep herself from checking on the time every few seconds. At six-thirty she got up and moved restlessly to the window, looking out on the grassy courtyard and gnarled mesquite trees but not seeing them. A slow, anxious feeling had started up inside her. Nothing could have happened, she told herself. He has just been delayed somehow. He'll be here soon. He said he'd come, and I believe him.

Anxiously her mind ran over the events of the night they had spent together, reviewing the words he had said, the look in his eyes, the touch of his hands which even in memory sent shivers along her arms and legs, trying to find a hint of insincerity. She was sure he had meant it all. And if he was late now, it was only from some outside event, a weekend tie-up at the Chicago airport, some business that had taken longer than he had planned. He would be here, she told herself. He would come.

At seven-thirty the doorbell rang.

She flew to answer it, flung the door open, and was in his arms, almost in a single motion. The world fell back into place, the tiny anxious murmurings of her heart stilled and were replaced by the familiar wild pounding. Hungrily her lips moved under his. Then her head dropped down to rest against his chest and she whispered, "I was so afraid—I didn't know—I was sure you'd come, but still I was afraid."

She could feel his kiss on her hair and the tight band of his arms locking her in, holding her against him in a circle of safety and promise. It would be all right. He was here.

She drew back and took his hand to pull him inside. "It doesn't matter, I was being silly. I just kept thinking all sorts of things that might have happened, but I wasn't afraid of anything really, except that you might not *want* to make it."

He pulled her to him again. "Don't ever think that—ever. I'll always want you, Lee."

Once again she drew back, and this time she looked up into his face searchingly. For the first time she noticed an expression of uneasiness, a look of worry and uncertainty. An answering uneasiness stirred inside her and she asked tentatively,

"Did you run into some problems in Chicago? Was there a delay of some sort?"

His eyes slid sideways, away from her. "No, nothing like that. Actually I've been back in Dallas for a few hours."

"You have! But why didn't you call—" she began, and then stopped. She did not want to sound demanding or insistent or like someone with fragile feelings who needed constant reassurance. There was an explanation and she would wait for it.

"When I stopped at my apartment in Turtle Creek to change before coming here, I had a call from Nikki." Moving restlessly away from her, he stood with his hands in his pockets, staring at the floor. "She said she had to see me right away and would I come over to the hotel. So I did."

It cost Lee an effort, but she managed to keep her voice casual. "What was it she wanted?"

He glanced at her briefly, then looked away again, sketching a gesture with one hand. She thought he too was making an effort to appear casual, not giving the matter too much importance.

"Mainly she wanted to see if the next recording session could be put off a bit. Say until Wednesday."

"Put off?" Lee echoed. She could hear the hollowness in her own voice.

"Yes. So that she could work on the songs some more, perhaps come up with some slightly different arrangements— arrangements that she could handle and that might showcase her better." He gave her a look in which indecision, hope, tenderness, all made an appeal to her. She experienced a moment's furious anger at Nikki North for putting him in such a difficult position. Yet in spite of her best efforts to contain it, the anger began to spread, to direct itself against him as well. Obviously he was still being manipulated by Nikki.

"But didn't you tell her that was a poor idea?" she asked, trying to keep her voice even. "I mean, you are the head of the company."

He drew a deep breath which came out sounding like a long

sigh of resignation, as though he were preparing himself for what he was about to say.

"No, I didn't. Because I wasn't sure that it was a bad idea," he said at last.

Lee felt herself beginning to tremble and clasped her hands tightly together in front of her. "You weren't sure . . ."

His long fingers raked through his dark hair in a gesture of exasperation. Even now the sight turned her heart over.

"No, damn it, I wasn't, Lee. You saw what a fiasco that session on Friday afternoon turned into. If we can make it easier for her, come up with something more suited to her, why not?"

She would take this very slowly, Lee told herself. She would not let it come between the two of them. It was outside of them. It was business. She would not let it destroy the fragile love that was still so new and vulnerable. She would speak carefully, weighing every word.

"Maybe it might be better . . ." she began, then paused and started over. "Do you think possibly we might come up with a better album if we did it without Nikki? Leave it as it is, I mean. Just Dub's voice, with some additional backup musicians, and then find new material for Nikki? You wanted to do an album with Joe Bud Garrett and Nikki together. Maybe we should start with that."

He folded his arms in front of him. They had drawn apart and now stood facing each other, the few feet of space that separated them looking suddenly like a chasm. A lock of his dark hair, slightly mussed, hung loosely across his forehead.

"That was Joe Bud's idea too," he said dryly. "I talked to him later. You and he seem to be on the same wavelength. I told him I felt it would be a mistake, and I do, Lee. Please try to see it impartially for once."

The implied criticism stung her. She bit her lower lip suddenly to choke off a sharp reply.

"I mean, no one wants to take anything away from Dub's reputation," he went on, spreading his hands and keeping his voice low and reasonable. "That's not it at all. But it's old stuff,

Lee. Its time is past. His name still carries magic, of course, but I don't see how we can possibly go with the songs as they are. And besides, from the standpoint of public relations, the album's been announced, it's been in the papers, people will be looking for it."

Anger was gathering inside Lee, forming itself into a ball of fire that was beginning to smoulder into explosion.

"It sounds to me as if Nikki must have given you some *very* persuasive arguments," she said, and her voice had a sharp cutting edge. He shot her a look and seemed about to speak, but she hurried on. "And what do you mean—its time is past? Dub Colder's music?"

"You're just getting your back up over this," he said coolly. "If you'd forget for one minute that you're his daughter and think of it as any recording project, you'd see—"

"Forget!" she shouted furiously. "Forget that Dub Colder was my father? I can't believe you're saying that to me!" Green eyes flashed at him. Her coppery hair seemed to shoot off sparks. His hands came up to pat the air in a placating gesture.

"Now take it easy. I didn't mean it the way you're making it sound. Of course you're proud of Dub's reputation. You have every right to be. But when something's over, it's over, that's all."

"People have never stopped buying his records!"

"Old familiar stuff, yes. Songs they know. These are eight new songs, Lee, never heard before. You can't expect them to catch on in today's market and take hold the way the old stuff did."

"Why not?" she demanded hotly.

"Because fashions in music change—like anything else. Today's buying public has a certain sophistication."

"Good is good," Lee interrupted stubbornly. "If it was up to you, I suppose we'd be throwing out Shakespeare and Beethoven too."

"That's a completely different thing," he said irritably. "If you can't see—"

"You're the one who can't see," she insisted. "Dub's music is part of America." Color was flaring in her cheeks now, her bright hair blazing in the room's soft light. "Just as much as Cole Porter, Rogers and Hammerstein, Hank Williams— they're all part of America's music and they're all going to last. Their songs will be selling when Nikki North has been long forgotten. And that's not one-sided prejudice on my part. That's fact. If you're too blind to see it, then you don't belong in this business."

"Possibly you don't either," he said curtly. "There certainly wasn't much left of the company when Cambro bought it."

"I take full responsibility for that," she said, and her voice had turned frosty. "I know I didn't handle things well. But it was only Dub's music that kept us afloat. If it hadn't been for that . . ."

His expression altered, growing regretful. "I didn't mean what I said, Lee," he said, his voice suddenly tender and contrite. "I shouldn't have said it. The company's troubles were not of your making, and I shouldn't have put it on your shoulders." He took a step toward her, but she backed away from him, her arms crossed over her breast, hugging herself tightly as though to keep herself from flying apart.

"Please try to understand my position," he said, once again driving his fingers through his disheveled hair. For a brief instant Lee, seeing the gesture, remembered how that hair had felt under her own hand, when her fingers had tangled themselves in it passionately, love for him bursting wild and unleashed inside her, all the world eclipsed in the furious sweetness of the moment. But the world had a way of reappearing, she thought bitterly. And where the two of them were concerned, there seemed no chance for happiness except in the moments when they were by themselves, away from every distraction, every other person, every mundane concern. They existed like dried flowers under a bell jar, she thought. Exposed to the harsh light of day, to the struggles and decisions of living, their love crumbled away into dust and all the old animosities reasserted themselves. One thought rose to the surface of her mind, bubbling and angry.

It wouldn't be that way if he really loved me.

And there it was, spelled out plainly, an inescapable truth. It was all one-sided, this attraction of theirs. She was no more than a diversion to him. That was all it had been from the very beginning. She meant no more to him than Nikki—perhaps even less. Because she had opposed him, given him arguments on policy in the company from the start, he had responded as if to a challenge. He had wanted to see if he could destroy her resistance. He had known—oh, how well he had known!—that sooner or later her willpower would break down. Say the right words, turn on the famous Cameron charm, flatter the girl. That would do it. *I'll always want you, Lee.* Even now, even tonight, he was still doing it. But for him it was probably not an effort. More like second nature, the result of a skill polished and honed to diamond brightness over the years of bachelorhood among the world's most beautiful women. No doubt he could do it automatically now, without even thinking.

"Please, Lee," he said again, his blue eyes holding her with those flickering lights like low-banked fires. "Won't you try to see it from my point of view?"

She stopped hugging herself. Her arms dropped to her sides; her shoulders straightened. She lifted her head and pushed back her hair from her neck. She stood with her whole body taut and unyielding before him.

"It's your decision to make," she said, keeping an icy calmness in her voice. "Do it any way you like."

"But I need you, Lee."

She chose to misunderstand him deliberately. "I'll be there, of course, if you'll let me know the day. I'm still with the company—naturally I'll do my job."

"Damn it, I don't mean that! I mean I love you. I don't want this to come between us."

Slowly and deliberately she crossed the room to the tiny kitchen that was tucked behind a waist-high bookcase.

"I thought we might have steaks," she said blandly, speaking as if to some new acquaintance. "And perhaps a salad. Unless there's something else you prefer—"

"Lee! Don't do this to me." His voice held desperation and a note of anguish. "Please believe me."

She turned to him slowly, wearing a tight little smile that kept her lips from trembling. She said, spacing her words carefully, "I will never believe you again as long as I live."

The words fell between them like shattering ice crystals, sharp and cold. She saw the low flickering flames die out of his eyes to be replaced by a frosty chill, saw his mouth tighten into stony hardness. A muscle just under his cheekbone moved slightly as though his jaw were clenching. He crossed the room toward her, walking with slow deliberation.

"Then this is goodbye?"

"Only in a personal sense," she replied crisply. "Of course we'll see each other in the office." She paused, struck by a sudden thought. "Unless this changes things. I mean, perhaps you'd prefer to replace me with someone more cooperative. Someone who yesses you to death and enjoys a bit of fun-and-games on the side. . . ."

Reaching her, he seized her shoulder and whirled her around to face him. A look she had not seen before was in his contorted features. Naked fury sparked in his eyes. His nearness overwhelmed her. He seemed to fill her whole field of vision. He loomed over her, towering in his anger.

"So that's what you think of me," he said in a harsh, rasping voice from which all trace of tenderness had fled. "Well, it's good to find these things out early, isn't it? But as long as you do feel that way, I might as well give you something to remember me by—something that fits your estimation of my character."

And before she could protest he had seized her to him, crushing her body against his so hard that she felt her bones would break. With one hand he seized a fistful of her hair, pulled her head back and kissed her upturned face, his mouth crushing hers so furiously that she could feel teeth, tongue, and hard sensual lips, all bruising and punishing her, all wreaking a vengeance that seemed to erupt from some long-held animosity. Gasping for breath, she pushed against his chest with her palms.

"Get out of here!" she exploded when she could wrench herself free. "Get out!"

"Don't worry, Miss Colder, I'm leaving," he said, and his voice was flint striking steel. He let her go, and she swayed backward, catching at the counter to steady herself. Her fingers came up to touch her rapidly swelling lips. Tears welled up in her eyes in spite of all the willpower she tried to summon up to suppress them.

"We must have another of these pleasant Sunday evenings soon," he said mockingly as he strode to the door.

CHAPTER THIRTEEN

The note on Lee's desk was in Ben Cameron's large, looping handwriting. The sight of it was a reminder of him, painfully intimate, but its tone could not have been more remote or impersonal. "Lee: We'll be in the studio this evening for another recording session. Around eight o'clock. Would welcome your input if you'd care to be there. B.C."

Still holding the note in one hand, Lee flipped her hair back over her shoulders with the other. Ridiculous, she thought, that this scrap of paper, this brief, distant contact with him, could stab so sharply at her. She had hardly seen him the last three days, and she did not have to guess at the reason. He had been spending his time with Nikki at the San Carlos—and perhaps at the studio for all she knew. Whether it was business or pleasure or a combination of the two, Lee had deliberately ignored it. She had not asked about him, had not reacted when she had heard Jennifer taking his messages or relaying them to the faithful Doris. "Mr. Cameron is not expected in the office today. I can connect you with his secretary if it's urgent. . . ." Not once had she inquired as to his whereabouts, nor had she reacted to the sidelong looks from Buffie, questioning and faintly distressed. Once Buffie had said, "Lee, did you know that Nikki—" But then the telephone had shrilled at her elbow, and when she had finished with the call, Lee was already busy speaking with an agent in her own office, and so the moment passed and she never did learn what Buffie had meant to tell her.

Now, tossing the note aside and picking up a pile of contracts to examine, Lee made a decision. She would not go to the studio that evening, nor would she participate any further in the project itself. The note had been oddly worded anyway, she thought. Not an order, certainly. Not "Be there." "If you'd care to," he had written. "Would welcome your input." It all had a remote sound, an implication that even if she did have a suggestion, it would not be a very important one. Last time he had been so insistent that she was needed. One conclusion seemed inescapable. Nikki had taken over the arrangements for the session. And if Lee did not appear, it was certain that she would not be missed. The note was a mere courtesy, cold and impersonal.

She left the office at five and drove straight to her apartment. It was a day of heat and strong Southwestern sun, and she headed at once for a cool shower. Stepping out of it, she felt curiously unrefreshed, and it took a real effort of will, once she had put on a light caftan, to make herself go into the kitchen, prepare a salad, and pour a glass of iced tea. Once she had gone through the motions and sat down at the small table, however, she did no more than pick at the food and sip the tea. Over and over her eyes kept stealing glances, against her will, at the kitchen clock. Realizing what she was doing, she hastily looked away from it and gave her attention to the latest copy of *Billboard*, examining the country charts scrupulously, looking to see what was on top, what was rising, what the competing companies were doing.

By seven-thirty she had leafed through the magazine twice but still had only a vague idea of what she had read. Words slid past her, jumbled, ran together. One article on a court case involving the piracy of tapes she had read three times; she was still not sure of the outcome.

Coming to an abrupt decision, she got up from the table, carried her dishes to the sink, and left them, then hurried to the bedroom. For a moment she stood there in the middle of the room, nervous and trembling. "Good grief!" she exclaimed aloud. "Will you please get hold of yourself, Bonnie Lee Colder? Will you start acting like an adult instead of a silly schoolgirl?" With deliberate control she went to the closet and pulled out a simple silk shirt and dark skirt. Nothing dramatic or noticeable tonight, she told herself. No preening in front of him. No feminine wiles—strictly business. She wanted to find out what was being done to Dub's music. She had a professional interest in the outcome of this recording session. She might have lost all control over it, but she still wanted to hear what direction it was taking. And that was *all*. The urgent pounding of her heart against her ribs offered her an argument, but Lee refused to listen to it.

The glossy new Cambro studio was too enormous ever to be truly crowded, Lee suspected, but it was already humming with activity by the time she arrived and slipped in quietly. An eight-piece band which had been set up and microphoned in the main room appeared to have just finished its work, for as she entered, she could see the musicians standing in a loose group, talking together informally, smoking, putting away their instruments. A short, stubby man in jeans and a plaid Western shirt was talking with them. There was laughter; people slapped one another on the back good-naturedly. It all made Lee feel curiously out of place. She had been through so many recording sessions, but always as an insider, a participant. Now suddenly she was an outsider and a mere onlooker, and she felt uncertain how to act. Furiously she reproached herself for not having called Steve and asked him to come with her. His presence would have been a prop and a bit of moral support.

Her glance went past the musicians to the glass-walled control room, where she saw four people in earnest conversation. She recognized Ben Cameron's tall frame at once, and again she felt that infuriating response, that sudden turning over of the heart even as she willed it to remain quiet. He was standing there with Nikki at his side. Her head leaned toward his shoulder and his arm was around her waist. Observing them in this distant way, Lee thought, How odd that men can transfer their passion so easily. How different they are from women. Remembering the closeness of their two bodies that night in the hotel suite, remembering the drive and urgency that had seemed to her a total commitment, she now marveled at how it was all dissipated, redirected. It had meant everything to her, but obviously nothing at all to him beyond one night's pleasure.

With an effort she brought herself back to the present, glancing at the two others in the control room. Ed Farraday—she could tell him easily by his glinting eyeglasses and balding head. The fourth person was a stranger to her, a heavy man, youngish, rather flashily dressed in a shiny shirt of electric blue. He seemed to be doing most of the talking, she noticed. The others listened and nodded occasionally. Ed Farraday, the only one whose face she could see clearly, looked slightly downcast, she thought. She started hesitantly across the floor, passing by the noisy group of musicians. The short man in the plaid shirt looked up and noticed her.

"Hey, honey, are you one of Ron's girls?" he called out over the confusion of voices. "Look, how about rustling up some coffee for us? There's a place in back somewhere where you can make it, I think."

Lee stared at him for a moment, speechless, not knowing whether to laugh or to answer him angrily, so she did neither, merely ducked her head down and hurried past. Well, what difference did it make after all if she was taken for somebody's hired girl, a mere gofer? Was she any more important than that, when you came right down to it? What did it mean, after all, being vice president of a company, if the title was an empty one and her opinion not requested? She headed toward a group of chairs against the far wall where she would be out of the way. Then, seconds later, she wished that she had had the decisiveness to turn around and leave the way she had come, for the door of the control room opened suddenly just as she came opposite it. Ben and Nikki stepped out into the main room. For a moment the three of them froze, no one moving, no one speaking. It was Nikki who bridged the silence first, and her voice was mellow honey.

"Lee! We didn't expect you. How nice that you were able to make it."

"Thank you." Lee could hear her own voice coming as though from a far distance.

"I'm sure you're going to absolutely *love* what we've come up with for your daddy's songs," Nikki said. "All we needed was a fresh approach. Isn't that right, Ben?"

"Yes, I'm sure of it," Ben said easily, looking away from Lee to smile down at Nikki. "Well, it looks as if they're ready for you, sweetie. Go to it."

The musicians were moving away now, getting ready to leave, their job done. Nikki let go Ben's arm and stood on tiptoe to give him a quick, soft kiss, then flashed a quick triumphant look in Lee's direction. Lee watched as she slid onto a stool in front of the microphone and slipped on headphones. The stocky man moved around her fussily, adjusting the microphone to the correct height.

"Glad you could make it, Lee," Ben said. "Wouldn't you like to listen in the control room?" His voice was that of a stranger, polite and remote.

Lee squared her shoulders. "That would be very nice. Thank you." She glanced around the studio. "Who *are* all these people?" she inquired. "I don't recognize any of them. I see you decided to use a different band. I don't even know them."

His eyes met hers directly for the first time, and their deep blue seemed to pierce through to her very depths. Longing that was like small tongues of flame licked along her arms even as she felt a cold stone of despair settle inside her. She should have stayed away, she thought helplessly. It was not Nikki's brazen flaunting of intimacy that got to her. It was seeing him, hearing his voice: those were things she could not cope with.

"They're all people Nikki's worked with before—in Nashville," he explained. "She felt she could manage better with people who were familiar with her style."

"Nashville?"

"Yes. The fellow talking with her over there"—he nodded toward them—"that's Mac Raines."

"The arranger?"

"Yes. Nikki's done a number of sessions with him. He's come

up with an arrangement for her—well, several, in fact, that she likes very much."

"Mac Raines is very well known in country music." Lee did not add her own opinion of his work—that she considered it for the most part ordinary and tasteless.

"The other one, the man in the control room with Ed Farraday, that's Ron Frazer, an engineer who knows Nikki's voice well. He's going to be taking over on the board, just for this album."

No wonder poor Ed was looking downcast, Lee thought. He was being usurped at his beautiful control board. And now suddenly it became clear to her why Nikki's resentment of her had faded away. Having hit upon this new plan, having decided, probably right after the disastrous first session at which Lee was present, to bring in her own people, Nikki was able to feel relaxed and expansive. Lee was no longer a threat to her. Not where the recording was concerned, and not where Ben was concerned either. The intimacy between the two was warm and unmistakable, and obviously Nikki's plans appealed to him, since he was going along with them—at considerable expense, Lee guessed. She tried to maintain a professional interest, to keep the conversation far away from anything personal. Yet she could not help confronting him with it.

"This was what Nikki wanted to discuss with you on Sunday when you got back from Chicago."

His jaw tightened in that way she had come to know so well.

"We discussed it, yes."

"It was all decided then, by the time I saw you."

"It wasn't any big top-management decision," he said stiffly. "It was just something we felt might work, something we thought might help to bring it off."

We felt. We thought. The words echoed bitterly in Lee's mind. Remembering how she had run to the door when he arrived, how she had flung her arms around him and melted into his embrace, she felt a hot surge of color mount to her cheeks. What a fool he must have thought her—what a love-starved, gullible fool. And it was true—she was a fool, had been from the very beginning, to think that a man of Ben Cameron's sophistication and worldliness would be interested in someone like her.

She saw him looking at her and could not bear to think that he might be reading her thoughts. She tried to sound remote and professional as she asked, "Then the band has finished? They've already put new background music on tape for Nikki?"

"Yes, they'd just finished it before you got here. A much fuller—well, a different sound. But I think it's going to improve things a lot. Would you like to hear a little of it while Nikki's getting set up?"

He was treating her with the cool courtesy of a stranger, she thought, feeling the heavy dead weight of despair inside.

"No thanks, I'll wait," she said. She was already regretting that she had agreed to listen in the control room. At the moment she wanted nothing more than to get away, escape, leave this place and never lay eyes on it or on Ben Cameron again.

She glanced over at Nikki, perched on the stool now with the arranger hovering near. He was talking to her, encouraging or instructing, but Nikki seemed to be only half listening. As Lee watched, Nikki looked over her shoulder and gave her a long look of derision and triumph, her lip slightly curled, her eyes glittering. Then almost at once her glance shifted to Ben, and her expression softened to an almost liquid sensuality, her mouth parting slightly to form an inviting kiss, her eyes under their long lashes limpid with desire.

Distantly, Lee could hear Mac Raines saying with enthusiasm: "Band sounds great, honey . . . a nice full show sound, no more of that lonesome cowboy stuff . . . and you'll be right up front. Your voice is what we'll hear . . . whole new concept. You're doing the singing, see. And Dub Colder's voice comes in with a reverb on it, as if he's helping you out, like. A heavenly voice coming in just at the end, that's what it'll sound like. Well, he is dead after all. . . ."

The room spun around Lee's head. Black spirals and circles

exploded before her eyes, and quite suddenly she knew she had to get out, had to leave before she did something foolish. She was feeling an almost uncontrollable desire to lash out, to strike, to wound. Yet she was determined not to give either of them—Nikki or Ben—the satisfaction of knowing how totally they had defeated her.

"Excuse me," she said abruptly. "I don't think I can be of any help here. You won't mind if I leave now. . . ."

"Lee. . . ." She heard his voice calling after her, or perhaps, she thought in her confusion, she only imagined she heard it. She kept her back very straight as she walked across the studio, not looking again toward Nikki, not looking back at all. She opened the front door and was out in the parking lot and in her car in seconds. She turned the key in the ignition, backed out in one swift turning arc, and returned the way she had come. Only not to her snug, small apartment and its painful memories. Instead, after she had left Cambro Park she turned eastward. Her foot pressed down urgently on the accelerator as she headed through city traffic to pick up the road to Sulphur Springs. Distantly she heard thunder rolling in.

Rain had been forecast all day. Now, in the thick heavy darkness of early evening, she heard thunder and saw flashes of lightning. She hardly noticed them in her impatience to be on her way. When traffic in Dallas slowed her down, she tapped restlessly with her fingertips on the steering wheel. Now and then she slid a hand to the back of her neck and pushed back the heavy hair that clung damply there. By the time she crossed Lake Ray Hubbard east of the city, the rain had just begun, big noisy drops that splattered on her windshield. For a moment, glimpsing the sheen of the lake below, she thought back to the day she had come here with Ben, the day she had acted as his tour guide. How lighthearted they had both been that day—she could recall every moment. The drive up and down Dallas streets as she pointed and explained and he drove slowly, not wanting to miss anything. Their luncheon in the little Greek restaurant, the drive to Fort Worth, the eerie sound of the wind as they stood close together in the old stockyards. And the slow, sultry arousal she had felt, the physical awareness of him so near her. Later, in her apartment, she had watched the storm—like this one—coming nearer and nearer. And when it crashed down upon them, it was no stronger or louder than the crash of her own emotions responding to his kiss.

She left the lake behind her and picked up the highway headed away from the city lights and traffic, out into the open country dotted with small towns whose names were indicated on the signs showing exits. If only, if only, she thought, and the words kept time with the swish of the windshield wipers as the rain began to come down harder. If only she could go back to that day—do it all over, she thought, so that things would turn out differently. But it would never work, even if such a thing were possible. She was who she was, and so was he. Both of them would act as they had then, and it would all come to the same thing in the end. For a moment she saw, instead of the rainswept windshield in front of her, that look Nikki had cast in her direction—triumphant, derisive, challenging. Almost as if to say, What are you going to do about it? Knowing she had won, knowing the contest was over.

For the fraction of a second Lee's hands grew slack on the steering wheel and her eyes squeezed shut and reopened. In that tiny blink of time an eighteen-wheeler sped by on her left, jolting her car with a shock wave of air and sending a sheet of water across the windshield. Shaken, Lee tightened her grasp on the wheel in a quick, instinctive reaction as she realized she had foolishly allowed her mind to drift away from her driving. An inexcusable lapse. She pulled off the road and took a few moments to recover, scolding herself silently and reminding herself with a grim reprimand that whatever had happened, whatever she had lost, it was unimportant beside the possibility of losing her life in a highway accident. At last she checked her seatbelt and pulled back onto the highway, carefully now and concentrating on every aspect of her driving. Traffic was thinner as evening advanced, and the rain continued to fall steadily through the blackness. She kept her eyes on the road in front of her, although the gusts of rain were now more than the wipers could cope with and kept dimming her visibility.

Yet even with the best of intentions, her mind kept sliding back to the decision she knew she had to make. Had she, in fact, already made it? Was that why she had fled from the studio and headed away from Dallas through this stormy night? To turn her back on all of them, and on the company itself? Was it time at last for her to quit WW Music for good?

A flash of lightning cracked the heavens open and illuminated a high water tower to her left and the lettering on it: FATE. Suddenly memory brought back that day at the new studio, with reporters throwing out their questions, flashbulbs popping, and Joe Bud Garrett beside her, easy and friendly. *I come from Fate. . . . You know it? Got its name stuck right up there on that big old water tower . . . maybe it was my fate to come home to it. . . .*

And what about my fate? The words echoed crazily in Lee's head as she rounded a curve in the highway. Then she gave a gasp. Dead ahead was the eighteen-wheeler that had passed her several miles back. Only now it was sprawled over the highway, jackknifed across both lanes. There was no time for thought, only swift reaction. Lee slammed on the brakes and pulled hard to the right. The last thing she saw was a sign illuminated by her swerving headlights: FATE—EXIT HERE.

She was vaguely aware of being lifted from the car and placed on a blanket on the wet pavement. Raindrops were hitting her face. Voices came near and then receded. She heard a siren, then at last she was out of the wet and lying somewhere else. Bright lights shone down on her and someone in a white coat leaned over her. Ben Cameron? No, it seemed to be a doctor. But was Ben a doctor? Was that something she had forgotten? No, surely not. She felt a twinge of disappointment. Then darkness closed over her with a stark and sudden finality.

CHAPTER FOURTEEN

In her dream Lee heard a confusion of voices and saw faces hovering over her. Yet they were impermanent, kept fading away, retreating, coming back. Some of the time she was actually aware of its being a dream and she tried to fight her way out of it and return to reality. Other times she slid back into the dream and let it take over. Voices came at her from all sides, some of them familiar, some of them the voices of strangers, and the words seemed to make no sense at all.

"Yes, very stubborn, of course. . . ."

"Can't imagine how she ever . . ."

"Excuse me, but this is important, sir. . . ."

"Where can I reach you. . . ?"

"No, no, I'm not leaving. . . ."

It all had to do with a mix-up at the office, Lee thought in her half-waking dream state. He was criticizing her again, obviously, calling her stubborn. There was some problem, something that had been bothering her, but now she could not remember what it was. Something had gone wrong, and it was her fault for not giving in, and now he was being critical. But who? Who was the *he* in her dream? Possibly her father, although it certainly didn't sound like him. And anyway, that was impossible. Dub was in the hospital in Waco, wasn't he?

She tried to move, but her arms seemed hampered in some frustrating way. She opened her eyes briefly, but all the images that greeted her were blurred and indistinct. Even Ben Cameron's face—that *was* Ben, wasn't it? No, she was wrong again. It couldn't be. Ben was so fastidious, so well groomed, and the face she glimpsed now, bending low over her, was unshaven, gray with fatigue, lined with anxiety. Definitely not

Ben. Then who? She gave a sigh of weariness and decided to sort it all out later.

"Excuse me, sir. You'll have to move just for a moment. . . ."

"I didn't know it was that late. Hadn't you better . . ."

"But why do you suppose she was . . ."

Why was she what? Lee wondered. She felt a small, needling stab, then a floating sensation, a soft drifting away. Why was she what?

She woke to sunlight, a clear, distinct light that looked like late afternoon and was real, not imagined, and the first thing she saw was a hat. An out-of-shape, ridiculous straw hat. Only after a moment did she realize that someone was under it, and the someone was her Aunt Bess, sitting beside her bed, watching her with intense, anxious eyes, her forehead furrowed with worry. Indeed, her whole face seemed about to crumple into weeping, but as Lee studied her, trying to figure out where they both were, the crumpled look smoothed out; Aunt Bess' chin came up and her mouth grew firm.

"Well," she said in her practical voice. "About time."

"About time for what?" Lee said in a voice just above a whisper, a voice that did not sound at all like her own.

"About time you started to wake up and take notice."

Lee moved her head painfully and looked around the cheerful room. Pale green walls, flowers. She glanced down at her arms, which lay at her sides connected to various tubes.

"Where are we?" she asked.

"Hospital in Dallas."

"I'm in a *hospital?*"

"Have been since last night."

Last night, Lee thought, trying to still the throbbing ache in her head. Something had happened last night. But what? And now it was . . .

"What day is it now?" she asked weakly.

"Thursday."

Thursday. And she was in a hospital, and Aunt Bess, who

never stirred from Sulphur Springs, was here in Dallas beside her. Then last night must have been Wednesday. And why did the idea of Wednesday night nag at her so?

Suddenly she remembered. The note on her desk in his handwriting. "Recording session . . . eight o'clock. . . . Would welcome your input." And then the studio and strange faces all around her and Ben's voice, polite but distant, explaining the new plan for the album, the new arrangements. And then that long, slow, over-the-shoulder look from Nikki, letting her know without a word who had won.

Lee closed her eyes, a feeling of utter defeat overwhelming her as other memories came flooding back. The road slick with rain, the eighteen-wheeler slewed across the highway, the water tower that said FATE.

"There was a truck," she murmured, still with her eyes tight shut.

"Yes, you went skidding off the road to avoid it."

"Is he all right? The driver?"

"Sprained wrist," Aunt Bess sniffed. "And I do not intend to waste sympathy on him. Although I will say he came to inquire about you."

Lee's eyes flew open. "Did anyone else come?"

"Oh my yes. Plenty of people. I counted three doctors and four nurses once."

Lee's heart went plummeting. But why did she think he might have been here? It was that nagging dream she had had.

"People keep calling," Aunt Bess said. "And look at all the flowers!"

Lee, not interested, tried moving her arms and legs.

"I don't think anything's broken," she said.

"No, you were lucky. Took a terrible whack on the head, and I wouldn't doubt you'll be black and blue all over, but yes, you were lucky."

"And you must be exhausted, Aunt Bess."

"Oh no. This is a real comfortable chair. I took some good naps." The older woman's hand came out to cover Lee's. "I'm real glad you came back to us, honey. I don't mind telling you, you looked a sight when I first got here."

"Aunt Bess . . ." Lee swallowed, feeling dryness in her throat. She moved her head on the pillow with difficulty.

"What is it, dear?"

"I'm leaving the company. I'm quitting WW Music." It was as if she had returned to consciousness with the decision made for her, out of her hands.

The room was silent for a moment. Then a soft bell dinged in the corridor outside as some doctor was summoned. Aunt Bess' eyebrows had gone up quizzically. Her mouth pursed as though she were thinking hard about it. Then she said thoughtfully, "Well, that decision is up to you. If it's what you think is right. . . ."

"It isn't Dub's company anymore, Aunt Bess."

"No, I suppose not."

"And there isn't any place for me in it."

"Are you sure?"

"Yes." She heard her own voice, gone small and weak. "I'm sure."

Later when her aunt had left, at Lee's urging, for a good meal in the hospital's coffee shop, a stout, friendly nurse handed her several cards that had come with flowers. "Get well and come back soon. We miss you," said one, and it was signed "Ben Cameron." Bitterly Lee recognized the hand-writing of the efficient Doris, who had apparently been told to order flowers and write something appropriate.

Later there was plenty of company. Once she was conscious and starting to feel better, Steve appeared, full of lively chatter designed to cheer her up. Joe Bud Garrett came on his own, laughing and shaking his head in mock despair at her plight and causing a crowd of nurses to gather outside the door and ask for autographs. When Aunt Bess indicated that she was ready now to return home, give the house a good cleaning, and prepare a place for the patient to convalesce, it was Joe Bud who insisted on driving her, and Lee could not help smiling to herself at the thought of Aunt Bess sitting bolt upright on the cowhide seat of Joe Bud's sleek Cadillac, her straw hat firmly in place.

Only when Buffie came to visit, bearing an African violet in a pot, did Lee ask in a roundabout way about the things that were on her mind.

"Everything all right at the office, Buffie?"

"Just fine. You're not to worry about a thing."

"No, I'm not. I know you're taking care of everything." She did not want to tell Buffie just yet that she would not be returning to WW Music. She could not face all the painful explanations until she was stronger and more sure of herself.

"Did Nikki finish the album?"

"I think so, yes." Buffie's eyes seemed to be avoiding hers. But of course Buffie would know how she felt about it, Lee reflected. There was not much Buffie did not see.

"You took care of those contracts I left on my desk?"

"All attended to."

"And I had an appointment with Dan Thayer to talk about a new group he's handling."

"Yes, he was in. I believe Ben Cameron saw him. Before he went away."

The quick turnover of her own heart jolted Lee. How could it still hurt so much, just hearing his name, when she had already made up her mind that it was over, that she was finished with the company, might not even see him again?

"Ben's gone away?" she said casually. "On business?"

"Oh—not exactly. I mean, it might have something to do with business. I really don't know." Buffie looked suddenly uneasy, evasive. Natural enough, Lee thought ironically. She wasn't used to lying. And what more natural than that Ben should go off with Nikki on a holiday after completing the album? It was a made-to-order occasion for celebrating, a chance for the two of them to be alone together.

"I'll bet Nikki's away too," she said, trying for a light tone but somehow failing.

"Well, in fact—I think Nikki is out of town just for a while." Buffie's tone was growing more and more troubled. "But Lee, you mustn't let it—I mean, this whole thing shouldn't—you have to concentrate on getting well!" she finished in a burst.

Lee, sitting up in bed now, nodded briefly. "It doesn't matter, Buffie. Honestly it doesn't. Please don't worry about me."

In deference to Buffie's obvious discomfort, she managed to change the subject and keep it on harmless, superficial topics for the rest of the visit. But when she was alone once more, Lee turned her face hard into her pillow and squeezed her eyelids shut, trying to keep back the tears, but not succeeding.

Not until Steve had driven her home and she had been at the ranch for two days, not until she had begun to creep around the house cautiously and to feel somewhat like herself again, did she bring up the thing that was nagging at her. One morning over breakfast in the sunny ranch-house kitchen, with her aunt hovering over her, pouring coffee and pressing another blueberry muffin on her, Lee said hesitantly, "I didn't tell you the real reason I'm leaving the company."

Bess Colder gave her a quick sidelong glance and put the coffeepot down. "Well no. Not exactly. Eat that muffin, why don't you? You're too thin."

Lee supposed she was. Somehow her appetite refused to return. Her mirror showed a little thinness under her cheekbones, a paleness made more noticeable by the flare of her bright hair around her face. She had dressed this morning for the first time, and had found extra room at the waist of her worn ranch jeans.

"It's because of that last session at the studio and what they did to Dub's music." Briefly she described it, watching as her aunt nodded her understanding. "I just couldn't stand it, Aunt Bess. And it was all his doing. Ben Cameron's. He could have prevented it, turned down the whole idea, but he didn't. He did it for her—for Nikki. It was the way she wanted it. It was all his fault, really."

Aunt Bess traced the checks in the red and white tablecloth with one finger. "Yes, I suppose it does look that way. You feel something dreadful was done to Dub's music and that Mr.

Cameron was to blame for it." She spoke slowly, thoughtfully. "You're sure that's all that's bothering you?"

"Of course that's all!" Lee answered hastily, wishing that Aunt Bess would for once show a little less insight.

The older woman nodded again. "Of course if we were being really honest about it, we'd admit that it was partly your father's fault too, wouldn't we?" Seeing Lee ready to interrupt, she lifted her hand to stop her. "Oh, honey, no need to get huffy about it. He was my brother and I loved him dearly, but we both know he never had a practical bone in his body. He was a bundle of talent, and that was it. You'd never have lost the company and gotten into this mess over the tape if he'd given even a thought to business. Those eight songs he left should have been copyrighted in your name and instructions left with a lawyer about how they were to be recorded. All well and good to make a grand sentimental gesture, tucking them away in the storeroom for you to find one day. But lazy too. Dub was always lazy."

"Aunt Bess! How can you say things like that about someone we both loved so much?"

"Why not, if it's the truth?" Bess Colder said in her forthright way. "Sweetheart, loving someone doesn't mean you don't see his faults. It means you see them and love him anyway."

Keeping her eyes lowered, Lee saw the sugar bowl, the cream jug, the glass holding teaspoons, all run together mistily on the checked tablecloth. She tried to hold back the sobs, to be matter-of-fact about it all. But her voice was thick with tears as she said, "I'm not going back there, Aunt Bess. I'm going to stay here with you at the ranch—at least for a while— and just think about things. I need some time to do that."

"Stay as long as you like," her aunt said, ignoring the tears. "And think as long as you like too. Of course when you're done thinking, there won't be anything much changed, will there?"

"I'm still quitting the company," Lee said stubbornly.

"Well, that's up to you," Aunt Bess said in a dry voice.

Lee found that recuperating at the ranch was not the quiet, peaceful process she had pictured. Aunt Bess led a busy, active life which Lee had completely forgotten about. She managed the ranch itself, which, although small by Texas standards, still had its share of duties and problems. She dealt with the hired man who helped out, but she also did much of the work herself, tending to the stock and the garden. "Just try these now," she would say to Lee, dishing out new potatoes she had just dug that morning. And in addition, she seemed to be the one everyone called in every emergency. She was always cooking, baking, sewing, answering some call for help from a neighbor or from the church. Lee became used to taking messages for her. One day during the second week of her stay there, the telephone rang just as Bess was headed out to the barn to help unload a delivery of feed.

"You take that, will you, dear?" she called out. "I'm sure it's Nettie Price. Tell her I finished the lemon mold for the social tonight, but I won't have a chance to take it down there until later. She can pick it up if she wants to. . . ."

Her voice trailed off as the screen door slammed behind her. Lee picked up the telephone and answered.

"Lee?" A familiar voice that was definitely not Nettie Price's sent a swirling dizziness through Lee's whole body. She sat down quickly.

"Yes?"

"How are you, anyway? Better, I hope."

"Thank you, Ben. Yes, I'm—I'm better."

There was a pause at the other end. Then: "Well, you sound pretty much like yourself, I think."

"Yes, I'm doing very well."

"Getting lots of rest, I'll bet."

"Oh yes. Lots."

"Well, we certainly miss you—here in the office."

"Thank you. Did you have a nice holiday?" She tried to keep her voice light and offhand.

"Holiday?" She could hear the hesitation in his voice. "Oh—yes. Very nice. Look, Lee, I don't want to rush you if you're still feeling shaky. But have you thought about when you might be coming back?"

It might be easier to tell him on the phone, she thought. Just a few words, wrap it all up, let him know she would never be coming back except to clean out her desk and remove one or two mementos that she was sure were hers. Yet perhaps she owed him the courtesy of a personal notification, face-to-face.

"Lee?"

"Yes, I was just thinking about it."

"I don't want to pressure you. You must take all the time you need, of course."

But why not get it over with? It won't get any easier, Lee was thinking. "Oh, I'm feeling quite strong now. Aunt Bess has been taking good care of me. Perhaps in a day or two."

"Maybe tomorrow?"

"Oh, I don't know. Well, maybe." The thought of it, of seeing him that soon, started her heart pumping wildly. She made an effort to will it into calmness but only half succeeded. "I have to see about renting a car. Mine's in the shop, of course. It was pretty badly bashed up."

"I'd be glad to come for you—drive you back myself."

"Oh no," she said quickly. "No, that won't be necessary." The thought of the long drive to Dallas in the soft intimacy of that Lincoln with its quiet motor, its buttery-smooth leather seats, was a terrifying prospect. Bad enough to confront him in the businesslike atmosphere of the office. But *that* she couldn't manage, she told herself firmly. She would make herself manage.

"Well, if you're sure," he said, his voice sounding far away and faintly wistful. Immediately Lee's guard was up. She would not be taken in again by boyish charm, by professional warmth. Mr. Ben Cameron, she had learned, was a master of the soft sell. Once, to her everlasting regret, she had believed him. It came back to her in hot needles of memory, the vision of that night they had spent in the huge custom-built bed in the Cambro suite. How foolish and vulnerable she had been then, how anxious to believe him! But time and wisdom had overtaken her, changed her, given her cynicism. She would never let her guard down again.

"Fine then," she said briskly. "I'll try to arrange it." It was the same tone she used in business conversations at the office.

"Lee?"

"Yes."

"It'll be wonderful to see you again."

The hand that held the phone clenched it tightly in a sudden, painful spasm, but the voice that answered was as cool as autumn frost. "Fine. Goodbye then."

CHAPTER FIFTEEN

Lee started out early for the drive to Dallas in the rented car. She wanted to do it before the heat of the day became too strong, she told herself, but actually the anticipation was so painful that what she really wanted was to get it over with as quickly as possible and get back to the ranch, to Aunt Bess, to country oblivion. She would have to make some arrangements about her apartment, she thought. Perhaps it could be sublet. She experienced the odd feeling of moving about in some kind of limbo, not belonging anywhere, as she contemplated pulling up all her roots put down over the past five years. Yet far back in her mind lay an awareness that the only reason she was occupying her mind with all these practical details was that it was a way to keep herself from thinking of the more powerful, immediate thing that was in the foreground, threatening to obliterate everything else. Seeing Ben Cameron again, and for the last time.

Aunt Bess had managed to put a pound or two back on her during her stay, but not enough to erase entirely the hollows under her eyes that still looked faintly smudged with shadows. They gave her a waiflike, ethereal look that made her not entirely recognize herself in the mirror and that caused her aunt to shake her head in an unaccustomed display of tenderness and say as she left the house, "I declare, honey, you look as if a strong wind would blow you over. Now don't you overdo, you hear?"

Lee smoothed her cream-colored skirt and tugged at the soft tie of her pale green blouse. It felt odd to be "dressed" after all this time.

"I'll be fine, Aunt Bess. Don't worry about me. And I'll see you tonight."

"Maybe the drive back's going to be too much for you. Stay in your apartment tonight, why don't you?"

"I'll be back," Lee said firmly.

Aunt Bess threw up her hands at such stubbornness and waved her off.

She had been dreading all the attention, the effusive welcome, the exclamations, the questions that she knew were waiting for her at the office. Yet when she arrived and pushed the door open cautiously, to be at once surrounded by well-wishers, it was the very confusion of the moment that seemed to rescue her from her fears. Enveloped in Steve's bear hug, with Buffie firing rapid questions about her state of recovery, with Jennifer watching mistily in the background and repeating over and over, "Oh, we were so worried, just so worried," and with even sturdy Doris beaming at her over reading glasses, Lee found it easier to pass off casually the warm handshake Ben gave her as he strode from his office to get in on the general celebration.

"Welcome back, Lee—you're looking just wonderful," he said.

Lee managed to look up at him and smile her thanks, making sure it was the same smile she gave everyone else, open yet unrevealing. What went on inside her at the sight of the restless, probing blue eyes, the slightly disheveled lock of hair falling forward, at the feeling of the strong brown hand clasping hers, was something she was determined to keep to herself. Never again, she resolved, would she wear her feelings in plain sight for him to see.

"It feels wonderful to be here," she said. "Thank you all for your concern. It's helped me so much." Her eyes slid away from his as she spoke, moving around to include the others. She went on smiling and answering their questions, feeling his eyes on her as she did so, but not looking at him directly again.

When she was able at last to go to her office, she found it in immaculate order, with fresh flowers on the desk, all the pencils sharpened, all papers lined up neatly. She dropped into her chair, put both hands on the arms and let her head sink back against the leather headrest. The effort of driving all the way to Dallas, the strain of the well-meant greetings, had suddenly made her weary. She sat there quietly for a few minutes, looking up at Dub Colder's picture on the wall opposite her, thinking of the things her aunt had said that morning over the breakfast table, that forgiveness was the true test of love. Perhaps it was. And she could forgive Dub his shortcomings. Could even face, for the first time, the fact that most of this probably had been his fault, just as Aunt Bess had said. But try as she might, she could not find it in her heart to forgive Ben Cameron. For all his faults, she knew Dub had loved her truly with a father's love. Ben had never loved her. He had been willing to use her, both in business and to satisfy his physical needs, but he had never loved her. And she, foolishly, had opened her whole heart to him. Well, that had been her mistake. And now there was only one way to remedy it. She had to confront him, had to tell him that she was leaving the company. She dreaded the confrontation, the thought of being alone with him. But here in the office would surely be easier than someplace intimate. She took a deep breath and put both hands palms down on the desk in front of her to push herself up.

"I'm afraid we tired you out." The voice from the doorway was low and concerned, but it ripped through her like a knife. He was standing there in a thoughtful pose, studying her, his hands in his pockets, his shirt-sleeves rolled back as she had grown used to seeing them, so that dark hairs showed on his wrists. A painful sense of loss throbbed in Lee's whole body. Yet how could it be a loss? His love was something she had never really had in the first place. She got up slowly and faced him.

"Oh no. Not really. I guess I'm not quite as strong as I'd like to think, but I'll be all right. Actually I was just coming to your office."

His face brightened, but then as he took note of her serious look, the brightness faded.

"Well fine," he said hesitantly. "Would you care to . . ." He made a slight movement as if to return to his own office, but she said, "No, no, come in. This will do just as well."

He took a step inside and shut the door behind him. For a moment he stood there looking at her, his expression a mixture of curiosity and concern. Worried, Lee thought, that I'll collapse on him or have hysterics or some other womanish outburst that he'll have to deal with. More than ever she was determined to do this thing firmly and with dignity.

"I've had some time to think, the last couple of weeks," she began. "About my life, my career, where I'm headed. And I've come to the conclusion—that is, I've decided that the best thing . . ." She hesitated, then said straightforwardly, "I believe it's time for me to leave WW Music. I think I'd be happier elsewhere."

Now his expression was unreadable. The curiosity and concern were no longer there, but he was looking at her with a strange directness, his eyes boring deep inside her as if seeking out some clue that would tell him more than her words had. Yet he did not appear flustered or at a loss. He merely said, quite courteously, "Well, all right, if that's your decision, Lee, I respect it."

In spite of herself, Lee was surprised and hurt. It was probably a relief to him, she thought, but surely he could have hidden it a little better than that!

She said coolly, "Thank you for being so understanding. I'll be happy to help out in any way I can, of course, so there's no awkward transition."

"Very thoughtful of you."

Something was in his eyes, a glint, a light, a faint suggestion of—what? Lee was baffled by it. Not amusement—he was being quite serious and sober about the whole thing. And he was surely too suave and tactful to let his relief show openly. Was he perhaps only entertained by her formality, her offer to help? As if he needed her help—certainly he had not welcomed it up to now!

"Well then," she said, letting her tone indicate that there was no more to be said.

"We'll talk about all the arrangements later," he said. "And don't overdo now. You said yourself you're still a bit shaky. Oh, and be sure to give my regards to your aunt, will you?"

"Yes, of course," she said, but then, as the door closed behind him, she added to the empty room, "To my *aunt?*"

She sank down into her chair once more, but the tiredness she had felt earlier seemed to be dissipating. She was restless now, full of an energy she had lacked only moments ago. Frowning, she got up and walked to the window, returned, and circled the desk twice. Then, making a decision, she picked up the telephone and dialed. When a familiar voice answered, she said, "Aunt Bess?"

"Hello, honey! How are you feeling?"

"Fine. Just fine."

"You're in the office?"

"Yes. Aunt Bess—"

"I'll bet everyone was glad to see you."

"Aunt Bess, have you ever met Ben Cameron?"

The silence at the other end of the line was brief. Then Bess Colder replied in her crisp way, "Yes. Why?"

"He sent you his regards," Lee said slowly. "When did you meet?"

Once again there was the hesitation, but again it was short.

"Why, the night of your accident. When he drove out here to the house."

"To the *ranch?*"

"Yes. You see, the state police had called him. Because of papers they'd found in your car—things with the company name on them. And of course there'd been so much publicity about his buying WW Music, they all knew his name. So they got in touch with him."

"But why didn't he just phone you?"

"Why, I suppose he thought it would be a shock to me, that it would be easier on me if he told me in person. Which was true. He was very kind about it. And then there was the business of getting me to the hospital, you see."

"He drove you to the hospital." This time it was not a question.

"Yes, in that lovely car of his. It was a great comfort to me, being so well looked after, I'll tell you. You had us all pretty scared, you know."

A hundred miles through the night, just to make sure an old lady did not receive bad news on the telephone. And a hundred miles back.

"Did he come to the hospital with you?"

"Oh of course. He was there the whole time. Well, there now. I wasn't supposed to tell you, but I imagine you've guessed by now."

"The whole *time?*"

"Yes. All that night and the next day. Well, shoot, he was there when you finally came around. Out in the corridor he was, just outside the door. He wouldn't leave until he knew you were all right."

The dream came back to her suddenly. The face leaning over close to hers, the haggard, unshaven look.

". . . didn't sleep at all, I don't believe," Aunt Bess was saying. "I dozed off now and then, but I don't think he did." There was a long pause, and the faint hum of the open line. "A very nice man, I thought," Aunt Bess said. "He seemed so caring. Caring! Well, I guess that's too mild for what he was. Beside himself, more like it."

"Thanks, Aunt Bess. See you tonight." Lee put the phone back in its cradle quickly, not wanting to hear more.

For a moment she stood there, joy surging through her like adrenaline. All those hours when she had lain unconscious or barely conscious. All those dreaming hours when she had imagined, or thought she imagined, him there. It had been real. All of it! He had been there beside her. He had cared; he had worried. *Beside himself, more like it*, Aunt Bess had said.

Suddenly she felt she had to see him, speak with him, tell him she knew.

She got as far as the door before common sense overtook her. What had he done, really, that any kind friend would not have done? Steve would have done the same thing, wouldn't he? Who could have seen Aunt Bess in her housedress and straw hat, anxious and worried in the impersonal atmosphere of a big hospital and not stayed around to offer support? It had no meaning beyond that. Certainly it did not represent any pledge of undying love. And once he knew she was awake and recovering, he had left lightheartedly for a few days' rest and relaxation with Nikki North.

Lee stood there, her hand on the doorknob, willing her painfully throbbing heart to cease its pounding, for composure to return. When she was sure she was in control of herself, she turned the knob and left her office. Nothing had changed, nothing was any different between them, but surely she should thank him, convey her gratitude for his kindness to Aunt Bess. She hated the idea that she was obligated to him and had not acknowledged it with any sort of thanks.

Doris, at her desk outside his door, was busy at the telephone. She glanced up and saw Lee.

"Oh, Miss Colder. Mr. Cameron just asked me to put through a call to Cambro's Chicago office. But if there's something—"

The door opened suddenly and Ben said, "I think I'll wait with that call, Doris, if you'll—" He saw Lee and stopped short. A faint color brushed his cheekbones. "Lee? Were you coming to see me?"

"I won't keep you," she said, marveling to herself at the brisk, impersonal sound of her voice. She was growing very good at this business of deception, she thought, adding the bitter postscript, it was something she had learned from Ben Cameron.

"Come on in." He held the door open wide for her.

She preceded him into the room, crossing the plush carpet and finding herself unexpectedly bombarded with memory.

That first day of his arrival, a day early. She and Buffie unpacking the lamps that had come from Neiman's. Buffie admiring them, she grumbling about it all, being critical of his expensive tastes. Now somehow it had already lost its newness. It had a lived-in look, the paintings blending into the walls, the big desk covered with papers. It looked like him, she thought, casual and elegant—right, somehow. She hurried to say something that would set a light tone.

"I thought all the best executives had clean desks," she observed, motioning toward the litter on his. "Isn't that the rule? Not a scrap of paper in sight?"

"Oh, I'm sure it is," he replied easily. He had strolled across to the window and now stood there in an easy posture, his arms folded in front of him, his weight resting on one leg. "Only where this company is concerned, you have to remember I'm still a learner."

He had never acted like one, she thought wryly. He had always given an impression of knowing. But no need to rake all that over again. She was still leaving the company; nothing had changed.

"I wanted to thank you," she said, getting the words out with some difficulty in spite of her good intentions. "I've spoken with my aunt, and she did at last tell me how very kind you were to her the night of the accident."

"You weren't supposed to be told."

She gave him a cool look. "I can't think why not. It was very generous and thoughtful of you. No reason to keep it a secret, was there?"

He shrugged and walked to his desk, standing near it and looking across at her. "Only that I didn't want you to be pressured by it."

"Pressured!"

"Well—I guessed that you might be thinking about quitting the company. I saw it in your face that last night at the studio." His mouth tightened, but he went on quickly. "That had to be your decision. I didn't want you to feel influenced by the fact that I was there to help out when you—when your aunt needed it."

"No, of course not," she said curtly. "I do understand. One thing had nothing to do with the other. And my decision isn't changed. I am still leaving WW Music."

Again there was the slight lift of his broad shoulders. The faint movement sent a tremor through Lee. The intimacy of it, the memory it evoked of the smooth, rippling strength of muscle in those shoulders, those arms, sent a soft, prickling tingle of desire shivering through her body.

He was looking hard at her, blue eyes probing green ones. "I presume you have your reasons," he said quietly. "I won't try to talk you out of it."

"Thank you for that. Because if you did, it would be just—"

"Hypocrisy? I'm sure that's what you're thinking."

"I wouldn't have used that word."

"You would if you told the truth."

"But I do tell the truth," she flared hotly. "And the truth is this just isn't my kind of company anymore. It's as simple as that."

He seemed about to rap out a reply but thought better of it. His mouth tensed again, then relaxed a little as he said, "As I say, you have your reasons, I'm sure." He came around the desk and stood before her. She had to tilt her head up to return his look now. Not really meaning to, she took a cautious backward step. "But would you do one thing for me first?" he asked.

She studied his face, trying to read it. Puzzled, she replied, "I said I would—I mean, help out in any way I can before I leave."

"No, I mean right now. Today. Oh, I know it's your first day back and all that, but it won't require any effort on your part."

Lee's heart dropped heavily. It was foolish of her, of course, to think that her impending departure from the company would affect him in any way. But for him to be so offhand about it—to be thinking only of some last-minute help she could give him, certainly indicated a supreme indifference. Still, she supposed she owed him something.

He seemed to be reading her mind. "You don't owe me a thing," he said quickly. "Only if you wouldn't mind too much —I mean, I would appreciate it."

"Of course. I'll be glad to," she murmured. Even to her own ears her voice carried the sound of defeat.

"Good," he said briskly. "We'll drive there in my car."

"Drive where?" she demanded.

"To the studio."

She started to protest, to question, but he was already at the door, holding it open for her, his face unreadable but full of purpose. As she preceded him out of his private office, she felt bewilderment laced with a kind of dull acceptance. What did it matter after all?

He was solicitous as he helped her into the car and managed, all the way to Cambro Park, to keep up a light, inconsequential conversation. Once he asked her if she wanted the air-conditioning turned higher. She said she was quite comfortable. They might have been any two casual acquaintances. Not until they pulled into the parking area outside the studio did realization strike Lee, and then she felt a cold shiver of dread and resentment that reached into her very bones. He wanted her to hear the tape. He wanted to play the result of the last session with Nikki for her. To gloat, to crow—oh, all very tactfully, of course. He wanted to let her know that he had been right all along, to show her tangible proof of how he could get along quite well without her in the company.

The tremor of resentment turned hard as stone and lodged somewhere under her heart. She had neither the strength nor the inclination for an argument with him, but she would never be able to keep her opinion to herself. The big, glossy band, the unforgivable manipulation of Dub's music—above all, the presence of Nikki on the tape quite overshadowing Dub, were not things she could let pass with a casual smile and a compliment.

As they went in the door, she inquired cautiously, "Am I to hear something?"

"Yes, exactly." He took her elbow and guided her across the floor toward the glassed-in control room. The place was a huge, cool cavern, silent and remote from the busy outdoors of traffic and heat. Outside the control room she stopped and faced him.

"It's the tape, isn't it? Dub's songs?"

"Do you mind so much? I only want you to listen with an open mind."

"But you're going to want my opinion."

"Which you've already formed without hearing it?" There was a hint of mockery in his voice and one eyebrow went up in that sardonic look she remembered.

"All right. I'll listen. Only I want to make it clear ahead of time that what I say will be what I really feel. I'm not going to pretend, just to be polite."

The blue eyes squinted with amusement. "I don't seem to recall your ever doing that in the past. Why should you start now?"

She was about to make an angry retort, but Ed Farraday, inside the control room, had spotted them and hurried over to open the door for them.

"Lee! Welcome back. Morning, Ben. Glad you're on time. We have a group coming in later to record, but I have the tape set up for you."

Lee shot Ben an angry look. So this last "favor" she was to do for him had been prearranged. He had anticipated every-thing, including, probably, her resignation. And this final twist was merely a turn of the knife in the wound. Her mouth grew straight with bitterness, fixed and unsmiling.

"Great," Ben said. "Let's have it, Ed. Here, Lee. Sit and make yourself comfortable." He pulled out one of the luxuri-ous leather chairs for her as Ed moved to turn dials and make adjustments on the big board.

"You won't mind if I turn this thing on and leave you for a

few minutes, will you?" Ed said. "I'm doing some work back in the office."

"Perfectly all right," Ben said smoothly, and Lee thought, *That* was probably prearranged too.

"Okay. There you are. Call if you need me."

He was gone as the first sound issued from the big speakers. Lee sat rigid in the chair Ben had offered her, but he did not sit. He stood near the control board, a little removed from her, his hands loosely crossed in front of him in that familiar pose.

The plaintive notes of a single guitar sounded in the wood-paneled room, a short, simple introduction with a familiar voice coming in: "Packed my guitar, and here's my fare; just give me a ticket to anywhere. . . ." Other instruments blended in behind the vocal. Another guitar, a drummer holding a steady rhythm, a steel sliding in and out and over the main theme.

"That's Dub," Lee whispered, and raised her eyes, frowning in bewilderment. "And that band behind him. How on earth— that's Willy Best, that other guitar. And nobody plays the steel that way except Bubba Franklin."

"Wait a minute now. Recognize the fiddle?"

It came in easily, unobtrusively, carrying the melody into the song's bridge and then dropping back. "Marty Hastings," she said in wonderment. "And isn't that Bobby Rogers on drums?"

"It is," he said. "Bobby was the toughest. Minnesota."

She stared at him, having not even the remotest idea what he was talking about, but for the moment not caring either. It was enough to sit and listen, to hear the familiar voice and style, the matchless perfection that joined singer and instrumentalists into one flawless performance.

Song slid into song, happy up-tempo ones alternating with muted, lonely ones, all blending into an essence that seemed to emerge as a description, a character sketch of one man. Not perfect, Lee thought. Not practical, and not always right. But himself. It wasn't necessary to be perfect, she thought. That was something she was learning.

When it was over, there was a long silence in the room. Ben reached over and flipped the switch off. Then he turned to Lee, already standing and looking at him, her eyes asking a question. His own expression had lost the confidence he had shown earlier. He seemed suddenly unsure, as though waiting for some sign of approval from her. "Is it—you know, what you wanted?" he asked at last.

She took a step toward him. "You know it is," she said in a small voice. "But how did you ever—and why . . ."

He put both hands on her shoulders and looked down squarely into her eyes. Lee felt a quiver of response deep inside, in her very bones, it seemed.

"Because I knew it had to be done that way. Because I knew you were right, Bonnie Lee Colder, and I was wrong. And I'll tell you something else. I knew it even before that last session. And if I hadn't been so pigheaded and insisted on going through with it, letting Nikki talk me into that three-ring circus, you might not have gone tearing off like that and nearly got yourself killed. When I heard—when I thought I might lose you—God, I nearly lost my mind."

She was in his arms, his strength pulling her to him, before she had a chance to frame another question, utter another word. His kiss, warm and moving, seemed to envelop her, turn her whole body soft and pliant so that every bone and muscle, every curve, melted against him and became a part of him. When she could tear herself away, she asked breathlessly, "But how did you ever—when did you do all this?"

"While you were in the hospital recovering, and then after you'd gone home to the ranch to rest up. I waited until I knew you were all right. I just couldn't think about anything until then, but I could see that your aunt was a very take-charge person and I knew you'd be fine with her, so that's when I left town to find these fellows, your father's old group."

"I thought"—she stumbled over the words—"I thought you and Nikki had gone off together."

He gave her an unbelieving stare. "Nikki! You're kidding!"

"But you two acted so—I mean, I was sure you were having a big love affair."

His laughter filled the control room, bounced off the walls, and came back to her.

"But I told you we weren't! Didn't you believe me?"

"I—I wanted to believe you. That one night—in the hotel—I really did. But then after that last recording session I was sure the two of you . . ."

He grinned down at her. "Nikki likes a lot of attention, I'll admit that. And she puts up a pretty steamy appeal too, if you're susceptible. I told you before, she's a great little actress. But that's all it was. And as far as being susceptible, I just never was. I'd met you, you see. . . ." His look grew tender as he pulled her to him again. Her head rested against his chest. She could feel his lips touching her hair.

"She hasn't gone away for good, has she?" Lee said. "I mean, Buffie said she'd left." Strangely she found herself hoping that Nikki had not quit WW Music, had not gone away in anger. Quite suddenly Nikki no longer seemed a threat.

"A small display of temperament. She went off a little indignant, I guess, when she found out we weren't using her version of the songs. But Joe Bud went after her and talked some sense into her. It's patched up. I blame myself, actually. It wasn't the type of material she could handle. I was expecting too much of her. We'll still make an album with her. You can help us find some suitable material, can't you?"

"Yes, of course." Her answer came naturally, because now it did seem natural, all of it. And right. "But tell me how you ever located those men—Dub's old group. I haven't heard from any of them in several years."

"Give credit to Buffie's good memory. She was the one who steered me in the right direction. Two of them were still in Texas, so that was fairly easy. Willy Best had moved to Georgia; that took another day or two, locating him. As I told you, it was Bobby Rogers, the drummer, who gave me the most trouble. His wife had been left a farm in Minnesota. We had no address, and that's a fairly sizable state too. But Buffie made some phone calls and finally got a line on him, so I flew up there to talk to him. And incidentally I didn't have to do a selling job— not on any of them. When they heard about the tape you'd found and when I told them they'd be backing Dub Colder again, just like the old days, they jumped at it. And you should have seen the way they slid into it here in the studio. Not a fluff, not a moment's hesitation, smooth as cream. Bobby picked up Dub's tempo on those drums and never missed a beat. They all asked after you, by the way, and I'm bringing them back for a real wingding when the album comes out."

She clung to him, content merely to listen to his voice, to feel his arms around her, to know the safety and warmth of his love.

"Only there's just one thing," he said hesitantly, and at once she pulled back fearfully to look up at him, to read his expression. Don't let there be anything wrong, any flaw, any reservations about this moment, her heart begged silently.

"Joe Bud told me what you said about this record. That it should be just Dub Colder singing by himself, his old style."

"Yes."

"Well, he doesn't agree and neither do I. Now my opinion may not count for much, but Joe Bud knows a thing or two about music. He thinks—and so do I—that you should be on this record with Dub. At least on one or two of the songs— singing with him, the way you were trying to get Nikki to do— that nice high harmony that she couldn't manage. All right, you say you're not a pro, but a pro isn't what we want. We want that sweet natural sound of yours."

"Oh, but I—"

He put one hand under her chin and tipped her face up to his. "Just do it the way I heard you doing it in the shower that morning when I was leaning on your doorbell," he said with a smile. "And I don't want to hear any more arguments about the new technology ruining music, either. It doesn't have to. It can make a good thing even better. Which is what you're going to do." He paused. "Aren't you?"

She tried to find breath to answer, but he went on. "And will you stay with the company? And make an album of your own after this one? You're too good to spend all your time behind a desk. And marry me?"

A small gasp escaped her before his kiss closed off further conversation. Her heart soared with the wonder of it, and all at once she remembered the sensation she had had that morning after she had stayed with him in the San Carlos Hotel. She had looked out of the high windows almost into the clouds, it seemed, and felt that it was her personal view of heaven. Only this was a hundred times better because it was real. Returning his kiss with all doubts swept away, she hardly noticed the small click of a door behind her until she heard Ed Farraday's awkward stammer. "Oh, gosh. Sorry."

Lee pulled away and turned to see the engineer backing out, red-faced. "No, wait," she said quickly. She turned back to Ben, her eyes shining.

"Yes," she whispered. "Yes to everything. But right now— Ed, come back in and take over this board. And where are those headphones? Can you set up a mike for me? We have a record to make."